T0354610

SECRETS OF
LIFE

AIDA GETACHEW

Order this book online at www.trafford.com
or email orders@trafford.com

Most Trafford titles are also available at major online book retailers.

Printed in the United States of America.

ISBN: 978-1-4669-7011-3 (sc)
ISBN: 978-1-4669-6998-8 (hc)
ISBN: 978-1-4669-6997-1 (e)

Library of Congress Control Number: 2012922128

Trafford rev. 02/11/2013

 www.trafford.com

North America & international
toll-free: 1 888 232 4444 (USA & Canada)
phone: 250 383 6864 ♦ fax: 812 355 4082

Acknowledgements

Before I write anything else, I would like to thank God, not because he plays an important part of the dialogue in my book! Without God, there wouldn't be a "SECRETS OF LIFE" and I am grateful to him that I do not rely on charities and homeless shelters for life. I love you!

Second on my list of priorities, I would like to thank the hundreds of authors who are already rich and famous due to *great*—I must add—books, and who are probably unaware that they have managed to inspire a thirteen-year-old girl who, unlike most teens, does not run away screaming from the mere mention of "book" to write a book.

I'd like to also thank my father, Getachew, mother, Yamrot, sister, Eden, and brother, Emmanuel, for always being there for me throughout the whole, long process of writing my book. I can tell you now that writing a book is not as easy as it sounds, and I had felt, innumerable amounts of times, that writing a book was just not worth wasting my summer holidays and half terms on. If it even needs to be said, I have definitely changed my mind about it now that it is finished! Also, without my parents, I would probably still be writing the tenth page of the book. I can't imagine how long it would have taken me to finish my book if my mum and dad had not been there to encourage and support me to writing more. I would probably still be writing it on the day of my graduation!

I would also love to thank my millions of aunts and uncles and cousins, all of whom have individually inspired me to finish my book, whether it was by telling me I was the "family genius" or recommending books to me. I could write all of their names and list all of their own different ways of inspiring me, but if I did that, my acknowledgements would be a whole different book!

Another major factor of my sudden urge to write a book and publish it has to be the fact that my school, Kingsbury High School, and my old Saturday school OYA were a part of my daily life.

I still remember the day I was being interviewed to join OYA, and one of their questions was "What do you want to be when you are older?" I immediately said author, even though I was still a scrawny eleven-year-old, and I am now the ripe old age of thirteen. Dr. F (runner of OYA) then said that I had "better get started" if I wanted my book to be finished by the time I was 18. I started my plans for my book the following week. If I hadn't had that interview, I do not think I actually would have made a serious attempt at writing and finishing my book.

School has also played an important part in the process of me writing my book; we would be studying language devices in English, and I would make a mental note in my head to add in more metaphors and similes or something like that in my book. My English teachers have been great as well, even though I am pretty sure that they don't even know I finished my book, and it is eventually going to be published. Without knowing it, they managed to answer all of the questions I had about writing my book during one of their lessons.

My friends have been great too, but I have the same issue about writing their names down as with my family—if I write one person's name, I would be automatically obliged to also write down their circle of closest friends! Believe me, if I wrote all their names down, I would soon have the whole student population written, and I'm pretty sure I can't do that. Plus I actually want to be able to use my fingers after writing this, but I'll always remember the day I told everyone I was writing a book and no one believed me. Thanks, guys. I'm joking; you guys are the best, and I'll always be glad I ended up going to Kingsbury High School, the "greatest school for miles around", because if I didn't, I'd never have met all of you.

As you can see, if I was left by myself on an island with nothing but a laptop, notepad, and pen, I would *not* have been able to write this book. Thank you, guys, for everything!

CHAPTER 1

"Beryl, Wake up child! School's started! Oh, good lord, one day I think I will pack my bags and leave this madhouse. It's the first day of school, a brand new year, and look where you are—in your damned bed. I don't even want to know what the rest of the year will be like . . ." My mother's voice trailed off into the distance as she went to yell my older brother to consciousness.

Imagine hearing that on your first day of school. It's probably no surprise to you that the day that followed was not exactly what you would call a good one. I yawned sleepily, dragged myself out of bed, and opened the curtains. I turned around and made my way back to my bed, preparing to dive into the inviting warmth of my bed that seemed to yell my name.

That was when I saw the time on my alarm clock. It wasn't just my mother exaggerating as usual surprisingly. I had overslept by about an *hour*. I shook myself awake and quickly changed into the first clothes that my groping fingers found at the back of my closet.

I ran out of my bedroom, banging my head on the way out, and I skidded down the hallway and into the bathroom. I then proceeded to brush my teeth in record time, and then I literally flew down the stairs. I tried to get out of the house, but my mother stood in front of the door, barricading me in. I tried to get past her, but *no*, Mum wouldn't let me go—surprise, surprise.

"Don't even think about walking out of this front door without eating every single bite of food on your plate. You need your energy." Like that's the reason she wanted me to stay and eat. She simply wanted to embarrass me, and the most humiliating thing she could think of was me being late to school. How creative.

I was about to barge past her, head first, when she put her hands on her waist and placed her feet on each side of the door, making sure that escape was impossible. This house is becoming more like a prison every stinking day.

"Mum," I began to complain, but then my mum got that look on her face that clearly said, "Don't argue with me unless you want to fight." I figured I would get out of the house quicker if I just listened to her. Plus I didn't want to be the reason WW3 started. I ran to the kitchen with my mother following not too far behind and hurriedly poured out a bowl of cereal for myself while my mother leaned on the kitchen frame, watching me with a satisfied expression on her face—Cruella de Vil's twin in person. I am honoured. When I was done, I didn't even bother to say bye to "Mum". I simply ran out of the house without so much as a glance at the front door when it slammed shut.

I had just started running to school when it began pouring with rain. Talk about bad timing. Luck is seriously avoiding me, and I don't like it much. Oh well. At least I was getting the shower that I had had to miss.

I arrived at school sopping wet about fifteen minutes later, even though I had run flat out the whole way, armed with nothing except for a half dead umbrella. I ran to my English room where I was greeted by a dragon of a teacher whom I had never laid eyes on before in my life. All in all, this was not turning out to be one of my good days.

"And what time do you call this, young lady?" she asked me, even though she had a watch on her.

"Just look at your watch, miss. I'm sure that will help you," I blurted out without thinking—seriously? I hadn't even gotten to my first lesson, and I was already losing my mind.

Dragon lady just stared at me without blinking for such a long time that I began to think of getting help for her. She grabbed hold of my arm and simply said, "Do what's best for the world, honey." Guess I'm not the only person round here going mad.

She then stalked back into the classroom with her nose up high in the air. I honestly started to think that I had imagined it all when she turned around and winked at me. Finally! Actual proof that I am the only sane person in this entire planet. Oh my goodness, gracious me. It could be the other way round though. I slouched into the classroom and slumped into my usual chair at the back of the classroom, next to the class idiots who also happen to be my friends, JJ and Tamara.

"What took you so long to get here? Did you try and save the world again?" JJ asked me, sniggering to herself. If she had heard what Ms. Sparks had been saying, I wouldn't have been that surprised, but somehow, I don't think that's why she said what she said. She is just weird like that. I really don't get her sometimes.

3

JJ's full name is Josephine Jackson, but everybody calls her JJ. Trust me; she looks more like a JJ than a Josephine. I've no idea what her parents were thinking when they were choosing baby names.

"Seriously though, what happened? You took forever. Ms. Sparks looked like she was about to have a fit when she heard you knock on the door," Tamara said seriously. Tamara has always been the most down to earth out of JJ, me, and her. JJ has her head way up in the clouds most of the time.

I quickly told them about my crappy morning so far, although god knows why they would want to hear about something as depressing as that. I had gotten only halfway through my little novel when I heard a voice. "Aha! Miss Jones has something to say surely. Would you like to share your oh-so-dramatic life story with the rest of the class?" Ms. Sparks asked me, her beady eyes gleaming with malice.

That was when I looked her full-on in the face. That was also when I had the weirdest feeling, and it wasn't because she looked like some undead monster. I knew exactly what Miss Sparks was thinking. I felt as if I was actually inside her head. She was thinking about what she would have for dinner, how much she hated teens, a spot that she had on the end of her nose, and about a million other things, only I couldn't focus on all of them at the same time.

I looked away from her, breaking the eye contact. From what I could see in her face, she didn't seem at all surprised at what had just happened. In fact, she looked as if nothing had happened at all.

"Beryl Adriana Jones, you will come to this classroom at 3:30 p.m. and we shall have a nice, cosy conversation; don't you think?" She said to me in a voice that "chilled me to the bones . . ." That certainly wasn't what I was thinking, but I nodded numbly, feeling cold all over.

I walked out of the class in a daze when the bell rang a second later, signalling the end of registration. The rest of the day passed in a haze, and I wandered from class to class without knowing where or what I was doing. I could have been in China for all I knew. There was only one thing on my mind at that moment, and that had nothing to do with studying. It felt like only half an hour had passed since I had had Ms. Sparks. No wonder she is a miss—she probably scared all the men away.

Finally, the bell rung to show that it was the end of the day. I made my way slowly towards Ms. Sparks's office. It was then that I realised that I could hear a weird humming noise inside my head. I couldn't get rid of it no matter how hard I shook my head. Huh, I guess it's time to visit Spec Savers.

It was all too soon that I realised that I was standing in front of Ms. Sparks's office. I knocked nervously, not knowing if I was ever going to make it out of her classroom alive. "Come in." I walked in cautiously. This was just like a horror movie. I wouldn't be surprised if Ms. Sparks suddenly sprouted fangs and admitted that she was a vampire in disguise.

Nothing would surprise me. At least, that was what I told myself. I took a deep breath and reminded myself that I wouldn't say anything until I was asked to. That was before I saw the look on her face. Trust me; it wasn't pretty. Before I could stop myself, I had blurted out the one thing that I had vowed not to say to anyone in my entire life.

"Miss Sparks, I'm really sorry about what happened this morning. I swear on my life that I didn't mean to do anything. Please don't be angry . . ." I began to babble. God, I disgust myself sometimes.

"Beryl, I have not brought you to my office to hear an apology, although I do admit that would be quite delightful. I have told you to come here so that I can explain what it is that you can do."

"Oh," I said intelligently. I mentally prepared myself for whatever it was that she was going to say to me.

"Beryl, you are a very special young lady no matter what you or others may think. You have the gift of seeing into people's minds. It is a very peculiar gift, and it is very rare. You are what we call a seer," Ms. Sparks explained. I could only stare at her with my mouth wide open for a full minute.

"Sorry, but I don't think I heard you right. Did you just say that I was a seer?" I asked cautiously.God be with her if she believed in all these lunatic stories. Next thing you know, she'll be saying I'm a psychic.

"Yes, dear, you did hear me correctly. You are a seer," she repeated loudly and slowly, as if I was a foreign exchange student. For a second, I felt a moment of pure happiness, but that came crashing down when I saw a glint in Ms. Sparks's eyes that couldn't have been a good thing.

"No," I said, "No, you're wrong. There is absolutely nothing special about me. You're wrong."

I then jumped up in a hurry, grabbed my school bag, and ran out of the room. I could hear Ms. Spark yelling after me, but I can run fast when I want to, seriously fast.

I ran all the way home, even though I was panting like a donkey with asthma, my hair whipping me on the face like they were live snakes. I may not know everything but I most certainly was not Medusa. I think. For all I knew, I was a reincarnation of her.

I was absolutely furious. I had felt so happy when Ms. Sparks said that I was a seer, even though I'd have to be in a very fragile state of mind to believe her. Finally, I had something that separated me from the rest of my boring family. It dawned on me a second after she had said that I was a seer that maybe this was some sick joke to get back at me for being late on the first day of school. My mother was probably involved. I wouldn't be surprised. It was a strange way for a teacher to behave. I should probably sue the school.

I stormed into my house and practically flew up the stairs into my bedroom. I flopped down onto my bed; and, immediately, my eyes began to close like I had recently bashed my head on a metal door, and I was on my way into a vegetative state of mind. I fell asleep within minutes. I should seriously get my head checked out.

"Beryl! What is wrong with you children! You overslept again! I swear, one day, I will move to the other side of the world without you and stay there," my mum yelled at me from downstairs, the last part trailing off as she muttered to herself how we might as well be mentally retarded. I may not have the latest gadgets, but I have a one-of-a-kind mother, one who cusses her children.

I sat up and yawned, rubbing my eyes with my knuckles. I could hear my brother walking down the hall towards my bedroom. He appeared in my doorway wearing just a pair of boxer shorts. I felt sick just looking at him. I should be put in therapy for looking at him like that. It's bad enough when he is fully dressed.

"Do you have any idea why your teacher, Ms. Sparks, phoned last night demanding to talk to you?" My brother asked, scratching his head—whoooo, new word in his vocab.

"What did you say to her?" I asked immediately on the alert.

"That you died in a car crash on your way home from school, and that she was invited to your funeral," he said and went back to his room snorting with laughter—idiot. He thinks he's hilarious, but, really, a barn yard animal is probably funnier than him.

I actually was late for school, so I jumped out of bed, washed, and ran out of the house all the way to school where I was greeted by Ms. Sparks. Great day this is turning out to be. I love my life.

"Ah. Beryl, just the person I was looking for. Come to my office with me, now," Ms. Sparks said in the type of voice that you would expect to hear from the leader of a boot camp. Even though I knew I was staring death in the face literally, I began to make up excuses as to why I couldn't go with her. Believe me; they were pathetic. A two year old could have done better. She just waved them away with a flick of her hand.

I just gave up on my free will and life and followed her without talking into her office that was just as plain and boring as I expected it to be. I mean, this is Ms. Sparks we are talking about. That was probably why her office looked so familiar even though I had never been there before. Now, I expected to see creatures jumping out from the corners. Ms. Sparks settled herself down comfortably in the big black chair in the centre of the room. "Now, Beryl, tell me why you got so upset yesterday when I told you that you were a seer. Most people would be delighted to be told what you were told," Ms. Sparks said.

"Well, not me," I said, feeling my anger returning, "I'm not most people. I don't care what other people would think or wouldn't think of me. Okay?"

Ms. Sparks simply stared at me, but I refused to look at her as I was scared that I "might read her mind" if I did and convince myself that I was more deluded than I already knew I was.

"What is the matter?" Ms. Sparks asked me in an unusually soft voice. Startled, I glanced up to find her looking at me with an odd expression on her face. As soon as I looked up, I felt myself being sucked into her again with no warning. As before, I read all of her thoughts; but, this time, I looked away as fast as I could, and I stared down at my lap. There was a silence that was broken by Ms. Sparks of course.

"Do you still believe that you are not a seer?" She asked me in that same soft voice, staring at me intently. I finally nodded my head, giving in. Besides, if I said I still didn't believe her, she'd put me in therapy faster than you could say yes, even though she's one to talk about needing therapy.

"Now that you finally believe me, I really should begin to tell you about the duties that a seer has to attend to. First—" she began, but I cut into her sentence before she could utter a word.

"Wait. Tell me first what a seer can do, or I'll go home now and pretend that I don't know you." I demanded, not caring in the least if I sounded like a sulky teenager.

"Well dear, I will tell you now, but don't think that you can just walk out of here. You are not the only one with powers," Ms. Sparks said with a wicked smile. I couldn't say a word, so I just stared at her in shock with my mouth hanging slightly open.

Ms. Sparks seized the opportunity to talk while I sat there in a shocked silence. After a few seconds, I closed my mouth, which somehow managed to pop open like some sort of spastic goldfish, and asked her the same question.

"Miss, you still haven't answered my question," I pestered her.

"A seer, as I once said before, has the power to read a person's mind, and, in some rare cases, they are also able to look into the future. They also see disasters and tragedies, as well as other visions. Their job is to try and stop them from occurring.

A person who is gifted with the power of reading the future would see an average of about ten to fifteen visions. They only occur when a major event in one's life occurs. However, it is not always easy to identify whether a person has both gifts. In most cases, a person who has visions cannot be identified until they have their first vision. They are valued very much and are spoken highly of. We call them psychics," Ms. Sparks explained, answering in detail.

I looked around the room, finally understanding why this room looked so familiar. I had dreamed about this room a week ago— ironic, really. It was almost like it was planned that I was going to see Ms. Sparks the week later, and she was going to try and figure out whether I was a psychic or not. The dream came rushing back to me like a flood streaming downhill. With a little gasp, I remembered everything.

I had been dreaming about something completely different when I smelled strong incense, even though I was asleep. I then found myself in a room that was identical to that very room. I was sitting in the same chair that I was sitting on now and speaking to Ms. Spark.

"What is it?" Ms. Sparks asked me urgently, alarm showing clearly in her eyes. I realised that I had closed my eyes while trying to remember. I was feeling oddly stiff.

"I think that I may have had a vision of this room while I was sleeping a couple of nights before," I said shakily. I sounded unsure even to myself.

"Explain what happened," Ms. Sparks said looking at me intently without having to look in my eyes.

"Well, uh, I was dreaming about something completely different when I smelled this strong incense that I'd never smelled before, and I suddenly saw myself in this office talking to you in these exact seats. I woke up soon after," I explained, not exactly sure of myself. Ms. Sparks kept silent for about a minute, staring blankly at the wall as though she was possessed.

"Beryl, it seems that you are even more special than I thought you were. It seems as if you are able to have visions in addition to reading minds," Ms. Sparks finally said, sounding dazed. Even though she looked like she had an overdose of happy gas, she still looked like she was hiding something from me. At least, I think she looked like that.

I couldn't be sure given that I wasn't exactly the easiest person to look straight in the eye given my little condition. I could only afford to glance at her once before resuming my gaze at a spot about one foot over her head. Of course, you could hardly blame me for brushing that little fact aside as soon as I realised the high points of being a freak. I mean, if there are any high points.

"This is *so* cool," I said once imagining myself winning the lottery and buying a mansion worth millions, completely forgetting that I would be lucky to see ten visions in my life. Plus one vision was down already, even though I don't see how looking at one of my teachers office while asleep is life changing.

Anyway, there was always the possibility that my mother would spend all of the money on herself. In my case, that was almost a definite. Ms. Sparks had to interrupt my day dream and turn my thoughts back to what mattered.

"Being a seer can turn out not as enjoyable as most people think it may be. Poor Tony Abacus was never the same after that time in Newcastle," Ms. Sparks said with a little shudder.

I was about to ask her what had happened when I was struck by an idea. I was only testing my skills, so there couldn't be anything wrong with that. Before I lost my newfound courage, I looked up, straight into Ms. Sparks's eyes.

At once, I felt that weird sensation that I was becoming quite accustomed to. It felt as if my body was left where I was sitting on the chair, but my mind was intertwined with Ms. Sparks's mind. Now, Ms. Sparks's was thinking about what had happened in Newcastle.

Apparently, a boy called Tony had gone to Newcastle on a school trip. He had seen a girl named Louisa Ellister attempting to commit suicide by jumping off a cliff while everyone else was in bed. Tony reached her before she had a chance to throw herself of the cliff and convinced her that killing herself was not the best thing to do.

Unfortunately, Tony tripped over and fell off the cliff, and he now has brain damage. Pictures of Tony and the girl Louisa swirled around in her head, and I could see that they looked like your average, everyday teenagers. I would never have guessed that one was suicidal and the other a seer if I saw them walking in the street.

Once I had extracted all the information that I could, I got the feeling that Ms. Sparks was getting annoyed that I wouldn't get out of her head. That was when I heard her voice in my head.

"Young lady, I have had enough of your poking around in my mind, so would you please be so kind and get out of my head," Ms. Sparks said with a steely edge.

I hastily looked away, not wanting to be in her black book. Ms. Sparks put on her designer glasses (and she thinks she doesn't get paid enough) and began typing away feverishly. I sat there in silence until, without looking up from her computer, she said, "Well, don't just sit there like some overgrown doughnut. Tell me what you saw in my head. I need to check that this isn't all some terrible mistake."

At once, I felt my awkwardness slip away like a blanket. I began to talk feverishly, trying to put my feelings into words. It was almost impossible. As I told her everything, going into the tiniest little detail, a question gradually began to form in my mind. I stopped abruptly.

"Ms. Sparks, how do you know so much about seers when you claim to be an innocent teacher?" I asked her with an intensity that I usually didn't have. She looked away for a second, trying to redeem herself.

"Well, I never claimed to be an innocent teacher, but I think it is time to tell you the story of me and my tribe," she said with a sterner tine.

"Tribe?" I asked, arching my eyebrows.

"Be quiet child," she said with a shake of her head. She then proceeded to tell me whatever amazing thing that had happened.

"Now then, you may already know about psychics. It is merely a legend revolving around my people. A very long time ago, long before dinosaurs were even thought of, our people ruled planet Earth.

We each owned a large piece of land. Some of us formed tribes and lived together in peace and harmony. Our tribe was called Consensio, which means harmony in Latin. This particular tribe was gifted. Each of us had a special ability that was unique to the owner.

Around nine hundred years after our race evolved, we were attacked. Our attackers had powers greater than even the strongest of our tribe had. Predictably, our tribe lost, and our attackers set about destroying our homes.

However, they didn't manage to kill the youngest of the tribe. Her name was Aya, which means, in the ancient language, she who lives. She had powers that allowed her to freeze time in a manner of speaking and carry on normally, but the rest of the world would be frozen around her. Aya was able to escape using her powers.

She ran away to a neighbouring village where she married and had children. Each and every one of her children had a power. They each married and had many children who then had children. Not every one of the children had powers though.

They became rare, and the people who had powers were very much revered. I am one of her descendants. There is one other gifted descendant, and she is sitting right in front of me." Ms. Sparks paused to have a sip from her now cold coffee.

I stared at her with my mouth agape, wondering how the person that I despised for as long as I could remember was related to a person who had powers including me.

Two things clicked together. If she was one of her descendants, it was only logical that she would have a power if she said so proudly that she was related to Aya. This seemed so unlikely that I snorted out loud just for thinking that.

"What is funny, may I ask?" Ms. Sparks asked me in a slightly cold voice.

"I was, uh, just thinking that, um, you might have . . . powers?" I stuttered, hoping that she wouldn't call a mental institute and put me in rehab. Instead of the sarcasm that I expected, she merely nodded. This brought on a whole wave of questions. I asked the first one that popped into my head.

"What power could *you* have?" I asked, instantly regretting my rudeness. Ms. Sparks didn't take any offense at my words surprisingly.

"Look and see," she said to me. At once, I looked her straight in the eye, grasping the chance to read her mind. As soon as I saw what she could do, I let out a little gasp of shock. I looked away, forgetting that the only way that I could read a person's mind was by looking them in the eye.

Once I had composed my facial expression, I looked up at her but not looking her in the eye to find Ms. Sparks staring at me with that same soft expression that I was sure that I could never get used to.

"You . . . you can make yourself and other people and objects alter their shape?" I asked, not really believing what I was saying, even though the words were coming from my own mouth.

"Yes, that is precisely what I can do. You may be wondering why you have powers when only the descendants of Aya were said to have powers. The answer to that is quite a simple one. You are one of the gifted descendants," she said using the tone of voice that you would expect a person to use if they were ordering chips. In other words, she was using a casual tone of voice. I stared at her like she had gone mad.

"No, I think you're wrong," I finally said, "That would mean that I'm related to you, which is not possible." She merely gave me a dirty look that said that I was the one who was wrong and not her. "That is all I wanted to say to you. You may go now. I have only two more things to say to you. If you ever see something that wouldn't normally occur, come to me at once." She said to me staring just above my head, careful not to look me in the eye.

I stared at her, waiting for her to finish the rest of her speech. She wouldn't move or speak. The room started to get colder until it was practically zero degrees. The fire was no help at all—it had frozen in midair. I shivered, and being cold was not the only reason.

"Ms. Sparks?" I asked uneasily, my teeth chattering. That was when I noticed a vague, bluish greenish mist coming from the mouth of the stuffed reindeer's head. I jumped up and ran to the door when it started talking in a deep raspy human voice.

"On the night before the Yule celebrations begin, great tragedy shall fall upon you. Loved ones shall be lost, never to be found again. Families shall quarrel, never to rejoin as one. Love shall be found, only to be lost again. It will be a time of great loss, and great triumph for those against you. The choice whether to end or continue this will rest upon your shoulders."

The reindeer's eyes seemed to grow in size until it appeared to fill its whole face. I heard a loud popping voice, and the reindeer's eyes shrunk as if it had all the time in the world until it was back to normal, and the fire began to crackle merrily again as if there had been no interruption, and Ms. Sparks continued to speak to me as though there had been no interruption. It took her a couple of seconds for her to realise that I was not sitting across the table from her.

"Beryl? I could have sworn that you were sitting across the table from me. How did you—" She seemed to be lost for words, so I helpfully told her what had just happened. When I had finished, she muttered some sort of prayer under her breath before turning to look at me with a gaze so piercing that it made me feel uncomfortable. She didn't say anything for a while, just stared at me, but I had to resist the temptation to look her in the eye and read her mind.

Finally, I turned my gaze accidentally on purpose and looked into her eyes. I felt the familiar sucking sensation, and then I joined Ms. Sparks in her thoughts. It couldn't have been too comfortable for her.

She was thinking about the last time something like this had happened. A boy named Billy Marcus had had a prophecy made for him in exactly the same way that I got mine, saying that he would die on the 30th of June.

Once he had heard it, he was too scared to go outside at all as he was afraid that he would suddenly drop dead. However, on the 30th of June, because of the lack of Vitamin D that you're supposed to get from the sun, he died.

Once I was done looking him up in Ms. Sparks mind, I looked away and at the door. As soon as I felt Ms. Sparks look at me, I spoke.

"I'm gonna go home," I said, preparing myself mentally. I've been doing that so often in the past two days that I'm probably an expert at that now. Unfortunately, seeing as this was Ms. Sparks I was trying to get away from, it was most likely that I wouldn't be able to leave as easy as that. Just as I had thought, when I had turned the doorknob, I found it locked. Jeesh, I might as well be psychic.

"Beryl, you honestly cannot expect me to let you leave now after everything that you have been through today," Ms. Sparks protested, arching one of her eyebrows.

"That is exactly what I mean. I need some space to think about everything clearly by myself," I said, emphasizing on the last two words. I could see that, without reading her mind, Ms. Sparks was getting ready to give me a lecture on how being by yourself was not the answer to solving your problems, but before that became a reality, I turned the key that was still in the door and bolted.

I had just slowed down to a walk when I reached the school entrance, and it began to drizzle lightly. Great, just my luck—I hate London. I was about to start running when I heard someone coughing discreetly behind me. I turned around to see a man who would have looked perfectly normal if he didn't have two huge black wings sticking out of his back.

CHAPTER 2

I stared at him open mouthed, not understanding why none of the people around me could seem to see him. I blinked hard, thinking that I was imagining things, or I was just going mad. I was just about to turn away and act as if I hadn't seen anything out of the ordinary when the bird-man spoke.

"I am no figment of your imagination. I am Ako, sent down from above from the troops of the Wrayalis," he said in a deep, manly voice that could have been music for all I knew. I couldn't bear to tear my gaze from his wings.

They were unfurled magnificently around his body and gave him an air of power that only a god or goddess could have. They were deep black colour on the inside, but they got lighter as it neared the tips until they were a snowy white colour that you would expect to see on angels. The only word that could describe them was beautiful.

While I was staring at Ako's wings, he was looking at me with what seemed to be growing impatience. I finally managed to look away and fix my eyes on a spot just above his dark head.

"It is acceptable for you to look me in the eye. Your abilities do not work on the troops of the Wrayalis," He said to me in that same deep, musical voice. I didn't believe him for one second as Ms. Spark hadn't said anything about my ability not working on certain people, but I looked him in the eye, eager to do some more mind-reading. To my surprise, the only thing that I could read in his eyes when I looked at him was smugness.

"You see? You are not as important as I am, and a lesser being is not able to read the mind of one such as myself," Ako proclaimed with a look of such importance that I instantly began to shy away from him even though I barely knew him. When I still wouldn't say anything, he gave a sigh that obviously said that I was just a waste of his time and not worth having his full attention.

I turned away from him and began to walk away from him. When I got to the middle of the road, I felt such intense pain that it shouldn't have been possible for me to still be alive. I dropped to the floor like a rock, and the last thing that I could remember was the sound of screeching tires.

"Beryl, wake up child! Yeesh! This child won't even wake up for her own mother. See how these children of mine disrespect me so?" a voice said, and even though I knew that whoever it was talking was right next to me, it sounded as if she was yelling down a long tunnel.

I opened my eyes unwillingly to see my mother's face so close to my own that it looked as if she had only one huge eye that stretched across her forehead. I yelped and tried to move, but I felt an aching pain in my head when I tried to move myself. I settled for squinting at my mother.

"Now you wake up! I've been going out of my mind in these last couple of days! How do you think I felt when I got a phone call saying that you were hit by a chariot and that I had to come straight to Morpheus?" My mother's voice blared at me like a foghorn.

I opened my eyes blearily, not realising what I was actually seeing until my eyes were fully open. Everywhere I looked, all I could see was gold. Even the nurses and doctors were wearing gold-coloured uniform. They appeared to have golden skin as well, but I was probably just going mad. I was lying in what appeared to be a king-sized bed on plump, golden cushions with a golden quilt, and my mother was sat beside me in a golden chair.

This room (if it can be called a room) was fit not even for a king but for a god. Knowing the way my life was going, there probably were gods here. It was only when I looked down at myself that I realised what I was wearing. I wasn't wearing my usual slacks anymore. I appeared to be wearing a hospital gown—surprise, surprise. It was gold.

"Where . . . where am I?" I asked while wincing as I stretched a long cut down the side of my face. I grimaced in pain, but that only caused me more pain as I contorted my face.

"You're in Morpheus, a hospital for the magically gifted." A nurse said, appearing out of thin air. I seriously need to get my head and eyes tested—Specsavers for life!

"Why am I here? I'm supposed to be in bed with Chuchu right now," I said stupidly. Clearly, I wasn't thinking straight.

"You see? I told you this girl is stupid," my ever supporting mother said, "Back at home, where you belong, you would be beaten senseless if you had been in this situation, but these pale skinned people do not allow this to happen. Did you do your geometry by the way? Education is the way to success. Without it, you are nothing."

I do not understand my mother sometimes. I'm pretty sure that being beaten would not exactly help my condition, but, clearly, Mother had other things on her mind. Either that or she wanted to give me a suntan of bruises.

To avoid World War Three from starting in the hospital, I simply ignored her. I threw my legs over the bed and stood up shakily. I was about to walk over to the door so that I could leave this mad house (make that mad hospital) when I felt the same feeling of intense pain, and I fell to the floor.

I could feel someone shaking me, but I didn't want to open my eyes and find myself on Land Gaga again. That was when I felt something wet fall onto my face. I opened my eyes wondering if it was possible for it to be raining inside a building. Anything was probably possible now if there were psychics running around the world. What I saw surprised me so much that I nearly fainted again.

I was lying in a hospital bed, a normal hospital bed that had curtains drawn around it. My mother was sitting in the chair to my right, sobbing quietly into her handkerchief, which covered nearly all of her face. All I could see of her face was her forehead.

I opened my mouth to speak, but all that came out was a croak that sounded alarmingly like a frog, but that was enough to pull my mother out of her own little world of grief. What I saw was enough to give any sane person nightmares. Her eyes were red and puffy as if she had been crying for a week non-stop. Obviously, as soon as she saw that I was awake, she stopped crying. Instead of barking at me like she usually did, she spoke in a soft voice that I had never heard my mother use before.

"How are you feeling, sweetheart?" she said to me while stroking the palm of my hand.

"I'm fine," I croaked through my parched throat. "What . . . what happened?" My mother stared at me, not wanting to tell me; but, from the way she was looking at me, I probably scared her into telling me. Oh well, there are always two ways to finding out things.

Just before I checked out how good I was at mind-reading, my mother spoke in the voice that she normally used. In other words, she barked. "Why don't you tell me what happened? I let you walk home by yourself from your detention when I should have come to your school and beat you in front of everyone, but me and my kind-hearted self let you come home, but look what happened!"

While my "kind-hearted" mother droned on about how irresponsible I was, I began to think if I could read a person's mind without having to look them in the eye. Maybe I just had to visualise the person in my head.

Before I could test out my new theory, someone knocked on the door. Somehow, I knew who it was even before my mother turned back into the grieving mother and said in a shaky voice for the person to come in. Yup, sure enough, it was some girl who I had never seen before in my life, but I knew who she was without her introducing herself, duh.

Adira walked into the room confidently, her long black braided hair swung behind her. She had light brown skin, and chocolate brown eyes, the way Bella from Twilight was supposed to have until she turned into a "bloodsucker." She was what I would call an exotic looking person.

"Hi, I'm Adira, but you probably already know that, and no need to say hello or anything because I'm totally used to people staring at me with their mouths open as if I'm an alien who came down to earth," Adira said with sarcasm in a voice that demanded attention. She sounded like one of those spoilt rich kids who always ended up being the baddies in movies.

She seated herself comfortably on the chair on my left and crossed her long, lean legs. I got the feeling that she wouldn't say another word until my mother had left the room. I cleared my throat uncomfortably, trying to think of a way to tell my mother to get out of the room without starting a shouting match that I would probably lose.

"Uh . . . Mum, would it be all right if I talked to Adira for a minute?" I asked cautiously, thinking there was not a chance in hell of my mother leaving the room. Of course, she made no move to get up.

"Of course, dear, go right ahead." My mother said, without budging an inch from her chair. Instead, she got out a book and her reading glasses, and settled back into her chair. I glanced helplessly at Adira who seemed to know exactly what to do. She stared at my mother for about five seconds, and then, without a word, my mother stood up, packed her stuff away, and walked out of the room.

Just before the door slammed shut behind her, Adira called out in a voice that made me want to do everything she said.

"Ms. Jones? Come back in about half an hour. Oh, and don't let the door slam behind you," she said lazily. How rude can you get?

My mother nodded mechanically before turning around and letting the door slide shut softly behind her. As soon as my mother was out of earshot, I nearly pounced on Adira with the most obvious question that any sane person would ask.

"How on earth did you do that? I've been trying to get my mum to do that for years!" I joked half-heartedly. Adira didn't take it the way I thought she would.

"You already know the answer to that." I stared at her, not getting a word of what she was saying, even though I could hear her perfectly well. She might as well have been speaking Japanese for all I knew. She rolled her eyes and folded her arms.

"Isn't it obvious? Anyone with a brain could have figured that out. If this is how you normally are, I don't see how you're still alive. I'm another of Aya's descendants if you even know who that is," she said slowly and clearly as if she was talking to a three-year-old. I sent up a silent prayer, thankful to Ms. Sparks.

"Yes, I actually do," I said smugly, "How do *you* know about her anyway?"

"Let's just say that I met a man who was supposed to be a good guy but, in the end, went rotten," Adira said vaguely, her mouth saying one thing and her face saying something different. I studied her curiously, watching as a flicker of emotions darted across her face.

She looked up at me through her long lashes and suddenly looked quite vulnerable for a second. Barely half a second later, her face settled back into her usual haughty grimace.

"Well, don't just sit there gawping at me like I'm a creature from the zoo. Tell me about yourself and how you know about Aya and stuff," Adira said, rolling her eyes at me as if I didn't know a thing. Next thing I know, she's going to stick her tongue out.

"Well, uh, I—oh!" I was about to continue, but I cut of short when I realised what that faint humming sound was. It had to be the sound of other people's minds. I felt something deep within myself stir, and I knew I was right. I savoured over the feeling of getting something right for once in my life. It felt as if someone had switched a light bulb on the top of my head.

I watched Adira's face switch from confusion to frustration to annoyance. She waited for me to say something; and when I didn't, she acted as if nothing had happened, and carried on normally.

"Well, what are you waiting for? Talk, woman," Adira said with the same little huff that I was getting used to.

"Well, my teacher told me what I was, all about Aya, and everything else that I know," I said, summing up the one day that counted for Adira in one sentence.

Adira opened her mouth to speak, but before she could, there was a sharp rap on the door. Before anyone could say a word, the door opened, and my mother walked inside, looking as if the world had ended. Something in her expression stopped Adira from sending my mother out of the room again. Instead, Adira got up and walked from the room, closing the door quietly behind her. That was when I got a good look at my mother.

Her arms were wrapped around herself as if to hold herself together and not break into pieces. Her eyes looked hollow and haunted. She sat down and curled her legs up to her chest. I was about to ask her what had happened to her when she closed her eyes and spoke.

"Beryl, it's your dad. He had a heart attack on a plane on its way to London. He didn't make it," my mother whispered, sounding half-strangled. For a minute, no one spoke. I felt something wet drop onto my arm, looked down, and saw a delicate-looking tear. To my surprise, I realised that my eyes were full of moisture. I blinked hard, wondering why I was crying.

My father and I weren't what you would call close. In fact, we were more like strangers. He had left me and my mum for some other woman when I was four or five.

The memories I have of him are always good, even though I could never forget the arguments that would start up as soon as my mum and dad thought I was sleeping, even though I was really hiding under the bed covers, waiting for them to shut up and let me sleep in peace.

I knew that my mother hadn't really stopped loving my dad no matter what she said. Huh, and adults say children are stubborn. I was just about to reach over and give my mum a well-deserved hug when I heard a vague little voice in my head telling me that my dad had been trying to come back to us. Somehow, I knew that was the truth.

My hold on my sanity became loose as I tried to keep my emotions under control and not turn hysterical when my mother needed me most. Great, I sound like one of those stuck-up kids who thought that they were all their parents needed to live a good life. As if.

A single tear dropped down my face, and I didn't try to wipe it away. I wanted to show my mother some sort of sign that I wasn't a human rock completely immune to emotion. I looked at my mother who didn't seem to remember that she was the one who was supposed to stay strong and tell me that everything would be okay. Obviously, with my mother, everything is opposite to what it should be, duh.

My mother looked up and gave me a little smile.

"Don't worry sweetheart. Somehow, we will get through this together and be strong. We still have each other. Never forget that," my mother said, giving me a strand of hope to cling on to. No matter what, my mother would be there for me.

*　　*　　*

"Beryl, Beryl, wake up," a voice said, sounding quite close to my head. I could feel cold breath on my face waking me up. My sleep-addled brain couldn't figure out why the person who was talking sounded so familiar, even though I felt like I had heard it for most of the beginning of my life. When the person sighed, I purposely gave an extra loud snore to further annoy whoever it was.

I felt something cold in the shape of a hand laid on my face, too cold to be a living person's hand. I couldn't resist the temptation and peeked a glimpse—Hell's bells. What I saw nearly made me shriek like a banshee and yank the duvet over my head like a little girl. It was my dad.

"How are you doing, my precious jewel?" My father asked me, bending over and kissing my forehead gently. He looked exactly the same as I remembered him—short with jet black hair and a receding hair line. His skin, which used to be a lovely honey brown colour, now had a vague bluish tint as did the rest of him. His body came in and out of focus, blurring slightly on the edges.

"Dad, what . . . how can this be possible? You died. But now you're here. Or I'm dead as well. But that can't be possible. I feel fine. But maybe dead people don't feel pain. Or . . ." I babbled on, trying not to let on to my father how shaken I was. After all, it's not often that a kid gets to see their dead father again.

My father's expression grew more and more sombre until it was almost difficult to look him in the eye. Looking him in the eye, I couldn't read dead people's minds either! I cut off in midspeech, sensing that my father was getting impatient. I took deep, calming breaths and pulled myself together. This could very well be the last time I saw my father.

"Dad, what are you doing here? Was Mum lying to me when she told me that you were dead?" I had already resolved to the fact that my stupid mother had been lying to me, and I was now planning different ways to kill her while she was sleeping. My father must have seen the anger flare in my eyes as he hastily assured me that my mother had done nothing but tell me the truth.

"So it's really true. You are dead," I said softly. He closed his eyes for a second, and when he opened them, they were full of pain.

"Yes, sweetheart, I am." I had never seen my dad like this before. He closed his eyes again, and when he opened them again, they were back to normal, but they had a sense of urgency to them. "I can't stay here for long. It's not safe for you to be with me," my dad cautioned, leaning slightly away from me.

"Why?" I asked, finding it so frustrating that I couldn't just zap it from his head. I could see a silent battle going on within my father.

"Well, spirits like me like the scent of blood, a lot. The longer a spirit stays with a living person, the harder it is for them not too . . . drink their blood," my father shuddered. "The only reason that I am able to stay with you now is because a spirit that has died in the last two days or less are immune to the scent of human blood."

I could only stare at my father for the next minute, trying to imagine him drinking my blood while laughing his head off. The image that I conjured was not a very nice one. In fact, it wasn't nice at all.

"But, it's still hard for you to stay with me," I guessed, knowing that I was right when my father flinched. Oh, wow. In less than half a week, I had found out that I can read people's minds, and now I was being told that my father could turn psycho any minute and drink my blood, so much for myths and legends.

"We are not talking about this anymore. I may be dead, but I would never hurt you. Over my dead body would I ever even *let* myself get so much as be tempted to drink your blood. If it does get that bad, I'll leave. And probably never see you again if I have to," my father said harshly, saying the typical words of an overprotective father.

I grinned in spite of myself. He sounded exactly the same as I remembered. That was when I realised that I would always be safe whenever I was with my father, even though he was dead and he lusted over my blood. Typical of me—trust dead people and not my own mother who I have lived with for my whole life.

"I need to go soon," my father said with a hint of urgency. I glanced up at him startled and saw that he was closing his eyes in concentration, and when he opened them, they had a strange calmness to it, which was the exact opposite to what I was feeling.

"No! You can't go! You just came! I might never see you again," I said hysterically, on the verge of tears. I mean, imagine never seeing your father again when you haven't seen him for more than half of your life already. That isn't something that any normal person would take lightly.

"Honey, I wouldn't leave you unless I had to. And darling, I need to. Being in the living world isn't dangerous for me. It's you I'm worried about," my father said. I stared at him in a gob-smacked silence, wondering if dying and then coming back had affected his mental stability. It probably had.

When I found my voice again, I tried to speak, but my father had taken my silence as an invitation to carry on speaking.

"I'm not supposed to be in this world unless there is an emergency that needs the living people notified." Before I could say anything, my father butted in once again. "I have to tell you something. You must swear on the River Hales not to tell the people I concern or anyone else for that matter. I am only telling you this as it is essential for your survival."

"Why can't I just swear on my life?" I asked, thinking to myself how ironic it would be if my father swore on his life, seeing as he didn't have one.

"When a person swears on the River Hales, it is binding—it cannot be broken. If you break any promise that you have sworn on the River Hales, you will not only die, but also your mouth will be sewed up with your own hands in the afterlife so you will never break your promises," my father explained.

To me, it sounded as if he *wanted* me to break my promise. Seriously though, what type of father would risk his daughter dying then having her mouth sewn up as if dying wasn't bad enough? No way. My father would never do that to me. At least, I hope not.

"Yeah, yeah, whatever, I swear on the river Hales." I said nonchalantly.

"Do not listen to a word of what your mother says," my father said dramatically. Was that it? I thought my father was going to tell me something more amazing like a cure for cancer. But no., all I get is a father that has trust issues with his ex-wife obviously. "Why?" I asked. Before my father could say anything, the sound of footsteps could be heard coming down the hallway. I looked instinctively at the door, and when I looked back, my father had vanished. Oh, crap.

The door opened, and my mother opened the door and let herself in. She seemed surprised to see me awake, but whenever she gets confused, she barks. This time, it was the same soft voice that she had been using the whole day.

"Are you okay?" my mother asked me, frowning slightly when she saw how alert I was. She was thinking that I was going to run away from the hospital. I would know, seeing as I was psychic and looking her straight in the eye.

"Yeah, Mum. I'm just, er, doing some extra revision," I said lamely, holding up my maths book that Tamara had brought earlier on during the day. The expression on my mother's face clearly said that she didn't believe me, but she just let it pass, thinking that I was having time issues.

"Well, sleep soon. You're going back home tomorrow, so you need to wake up early," my mother said with a long suffering sigh.

With that, my mother walked slowly out of the room, checking behind her to see what I was doing. When the door had clicked shut, I lay back and closed my eyes, trying to think about what my father had just told me.

As soon as my eyes snapped shut, I fell asleep. After all, how much can a girl take in without some quality beauty sleep?

*   *   *

I woke up at around eight in the morning; a feat that I don't do quite often. I yawned and stretched, wondering why the room seemed to be colder than usual. Of course, I had been visited by my dead father in the middle of the night. That was bound to alter the room temp, duh.

I could hear a vague humming noise in my head that was becoming steadily louder and louder by the second. There was a sharp rap on the door, and before I could say come in, the door handle twisted, and guess who walked in. Yes, it's the one and only—drum roll please—Acantha Evans! In other words, it was my mother.

"How was your night?" My mother asked briskly. Without even pausing to let me answer, she barrelled on. She was back to the soft voiced, sweet woman who cared about me, quicker than you could say "what's going on."

"Darling, you know how much I trust and love you," she began, giving me a sickly sweet smile that I had never seen her use before. "Sweetie, if you have any worries that you don't feel inclined to tell anyone, always know that I would embrace you with open arms no matter how big or small your problem may be. Now, is there anything that you want to tell me?" my mother asked me.

"*She knows,*" a voice whispered through my mind.

For a moment, I felt relief seep through me until I heard my father's voice echo through my mind. I turned to look at my mother. That was when I noticed a faint outline of green around her body making her look as if she was on green fire.

Before I could say anything, there was a loud bang on the door, and Adira came barrelling in as if a herd of wild horses were chasing her. Once again, my words were drowned out by the voice of Adira telling my mum to get out of the room in nicer language. I was just thinking that there wasn't a chance in hell of my mother leaving the room when Adira was obviously bursting to tell me something that could be majorly important or a juicy bit of gossip. Either way, they were both good enough for my mother to have interest in listening to. Surprisingly, my mother once again obeyed Adira as if she was the lord of the world and walked out.

"Okay, what is so important that you literally kicked my mother out of the room?" I demanded, hiding away from the fact that I was actually glad my mother had left me in peace for the second time in my life. For once, I remembered to fix my gaze on a spot above her head.

"I think I've figured out what the prophecy is trying to tell you," Adira proclaimed in her drawling, lazy voice. I really do not understand the way her mind works. How on earth did she even know that I had had a prophecy given to me? As usual, she completely ignored my question. My annoyance at her faded as soon as her words managed to sink in my stupefied brain.

"I think that the prophecy is telling you to beware of the Ulrika," Adira explained. Okay. I tried to look as if I understood what she was saying, but I obviously didn't fool her.

"You don't know about the War of Crivial, do you?" Adira asked me with a sigh. Before I could defend myself, Adira launched herself headfirst into some story about a war.

"The war of Crivial all began when a man whose name is unknown decided to bestow upon himself the honour of being the happiest man on earth. There was only one way to do this. You had to get the Scroll of Elysium and read it aloud in the middle of an orchard of roses in the dead of night.

He Whose Name Is Unknown's wife had already died in a car accident, and his two children had been taken into care because he had been abusive towards them.

There are very high consequences for those who take the Scroll of Elysium. For one thing, the Scroll of Elysium contains all of the happiness, luxury, and love in the world. If the person who reads the scroll of Elysium wants to, they can suck away all of the happiness, luxury, and love in the world until every single person on this planet is drained of all the positive aspect in life.

If the Scroll of Elysium falls into the wrong hands, the whole world would be doomed to a life of misery. He Whose Name Is Unknown tried to do what so many others had failed to accomplish years before him. He managed to do what nobody had managed to do before.

Obviously, no one in their right minds was going to let some foolish little man suck the joy out of life. They protested in mass riots, and, eventually, a war started. He Whose Name Is Unknown was by then the king of England, and he ruled quite a bit of Scotland and Wales as well. His empire was slowly spreading across the world.

The Kings and Queens of Africa, Asia, and Europe, fought long and hard against him, but as they had no happiness or a will in life, they were beaten easily by He Whose Name Is Unknown's troops. Three times they fought; three times they lost. As the kings and queens began to plan their next attack, word came that He Whose Name Is Unknown had been stabbed through the heart while he was asleep.

There was no trace of evidence to show who had killed him except for one little piece of paper with the words: 'Death is Inevitable.' People searched for the Scroll of Elysium for the next ten centuries, but there was no clue as to where it was hidden. All that was known was that happiness and joy had returned back to the mortal world.

The Scroll of Elysium became forgotten, and the war was forgotten in spite of the number of people who died, and suffered because of it." Adira finished of her story with a sigh of contempt. She obviously thought that she wasn't a typical stupid human being. She probably wasn't.

"*Okay*. What does this have to do with the prophecy?" I asked, wondering why while we could have been trying to figure out what the prophecy meant we were having a mothers' meeting about things that had already happened.

"Don't you see? This has everything to do with the prophecy. The Scroll of Elysium *was stolen the night before the Yule celebrations!* Without love or happiness in the world, families are bound to argue and never to rejoin as one. Loved ones would be lost as whoever has the Scroll of Elysium would be able to suck all the love from the world. The time of Ulrika was the greatest tragedy to befall the human race. For the people against you, it would be a great triumph but a loss of love and happiness for the rest of the world!" Adira proclaimed, her eyes bright with passion.

I continued to stare at her, unsure what to do next. There was no way that Adira was going to let it go lightly if I rejected her suggestion. It did make sense though. I mean, I didn't have any better leads to hang on to. I felt something deep inside me stir, and a soft voice whispered through me, "*She's right . . .*"

I started thinking that whoever had spoken had to be right next to me. It took me half a minute to realise that the voice I had heard was coming from inside of me. Great, now I was hearing voices.

I might as well be the freaking queen of weirdoes. I would fit in perfectly with them, no doubt about that.

"Okay," I repeated, unsure of myself. "If what you're saying is true then . . ." I trailed off, not sure of what to say.

"You still don't believe me, do you?" Adira asked me in a soft voice that I could barely hear. I couldn't say another word, so I simply stared at her like the big dope I was until Adira stood up without a word and walked to the door. She paused when she reached the exit and spoke.

"If this doesn't convince you that what I'm saying is the truth, then god help you," Adira said, throwing a piece of wadded up paper at me, clearly not caring if it hit me. Curiously, I smoothed the paper out with my fingers to find a website written there in large, looping handwriting. I looked up, full to bursting point of questions to see the door closing with a soft thump.

CHAPTER 3

"Beryl!" JJ squealed before practically leaping on top of me while wrapping her arms around my neck and almost strangling the life out of me.

"Let her breathe, JJ. It's not like she got hit by a car recently!" Tamara laughed joyfully before flinging herself around me and JJ. I could barely breathe by now, and my arm, which was in a cast, was wedged painfully in between Tamara and JJ's bodies. I gently tried to untangle myself from their bodies, but they held me even tighter. I was no match for one of them, let alone both of them. When they finally released me, I was gasping for breath and massaging my ribs.

"How are you? I wanted to come and visit you, but you know what my mother's like." JJ pulled a face and linked arms with me. JJ's mother is well paranoid about JJ. Ever since Mrs. Jackson got her last report, and as JJ is going to be doing her GCSE's this year, she has to stay at home and study, study, study. Thank god my mother's not like that about studies. It's only discipline that matters to her. Oh well, nobody's perfect.

"So how're you doing? Did it hurt?" Tamara asked me, signing my pristine cast with a thick black marker. Great, so much for keeping my cast clean.

"Did what hurt?" I asked distantly, daydreaming about life without JJ and Tamara. That just didn't feel possible. I looked absently around the playground, remembering not to have eye contact with anyone. The faint hum was back, and if I concentrated hard enough, I could hear the thoughts of the people in the large playground.

"Nearly dying! What else could have been more painful than that?" Tamara chuckled. Jeez, you can't get any less sensitive than these people, and they call themselves my friends.

"Oh, no, it was a walk in a park. It's normal for me to be in a life threatening situation. In fact, it's part of my everyday life," I said heavy on the sarcasm. Before Tamara could reply, the second bell rang, nearly giving me a heart attack. Abandoning our mothers meeting, we ran for the door as this wasn't the first time that we were late for form. No sane person would believe that Ms. Reggae (my form tutor) would let us off more than once in a school year.

We reached the door and pulled it open and ran to the English corridor. JJ and Tamara had had to go straight to form, but I had to sign in at reception, seeing that I wasn't at school for about two weeks. The entrance was deserted, so I left a note on the desk telling them who I was.

I was about to turn around and go to form when I heard a voice.

"*Be careful, my precious jewel . . .*" my father's voice drifted eerily from the corners of the room. I looked wildly around, looking for my dad, but there was no sign of him. I began to feel an unnatural breeze gently embrace me. It seemed to seep into my bones and drain me off my strength. The door banged open and I screamed in shock. To my surprise, I heard an answering shriek that sounded alarmingly like a grown woman. In fact, it sounded a lot like—

"Beryl!! What on earth do you think you are doing! Ms. Sparks practically yelled, sounding slightly out of breath with a look of shock on her face, typical. Trust me to go and bellow at the only teacher who had taught me anything useful in this messed-up school. Make that life.

"I was just . . . uh . . . just, um . . ." I trailed off at a loss of what to say. I mean, what would you say to a fully grown woman that you had just screamed at? I thought you were a monster? Pfft, that would not go down well with Ms. Sparks; that's for sure. "Well, you should be getting back to class now. And I am so sorry to hear about your loss," Ms. Sparks said with a look of grief upon her face. Before I could ask her how on earth she knew about my father passing away, she turned around and walked smartly out of the room.

I followed her and ran to my classroom knowing that I was going to get Hell from Ms. Reggae for being late for form. I knocked on the door dreading what was surely not going to be a good thing. The high, reedy voice of Ms. Reggae piped through the cheap wood of the door that the school could barely afford to buy. "Enter." I opened the door and stepped inside. Instead of yelling at me like I thought she would, she smiled.

"Welcome back, Beryl, dear." Ms. Reggae beamed at me, her dreadlocks cutting through the air. She ushered me to the back of the class, and I sat down, glad to be out of trouble.

"Now class, we have a new person who will be joining us at this school. He has come a very long way from Egypt. Would you please come up to the front and introduce yourself, darling." Ms. Reggae fluttered. So this was why she was acting all sickly sweet. We had a new boy.

A boy sitting on my right stood up and walked to the front of the class, not at all nervous. He looked oddly familiar, though I couldn't figure out why. I probably (hopefully) just saw him on the streets somewhere, though something was telling me that that was not why he looked like I knew him.

"Hey, my name is Ako." That took a moment to sink in. No way. It couldn't be. "I came from Egypt to see a very special person who doesn't know I am here." He looked at me and grinned. He looked exactly the same except for the fact that his once amazing pair of black wings was nowhere to be seen. He could have cut them off for all I know. The polite sound of clapping brought me to my senses and stopped me from day dreaming about wings. Pfft, if anyone could read my mind, they would think I was loo-loo.

There was only one way to find out if this was really the flying Ako who had nearly gotten me killed. I locked eyes on him, and, sure enough, I couldn't read his mind or whatever you people call it, although it wasn't that hard to guess what he was thinking from his expression. To put it simply, he thought I was bonkers.

He sat down next to me and took out his books without even looking at me. When he finally looked at me, he smirked.

"Remember me?" he whispered with raised eyebrows. What a jerk. He nearly killed me, and he's sitting there smiling with a grin on his elongated face. The bell rang just then, saving me the indignity of having to reply—*Saved by the Bell*. That program is so true.

I hurried out of the class, forgetting in my haste to wait for JJ and Tamara, and ran to the girls' bathroom. I locked myself in the cubicle nearest to the door and sat there panting like I had run a marathon. There was a knock on the door, and I almost had a heart attack, thinking that it was Ako. But then, Ako wasn't a girl, so

him going into the girls' toilets would be more than a little strange.
I opened the door, feeling all hot and flushed. Guess what? It was
Ako.

"What are you doing here? This is a girls' toilet in case you
haven't noticed," I asked in shock. I could feel my blush returning
slowly but surely as Ako was standing in front of me, which was
quite frankly impossible.

"I know it is," Ako said smugly. "But no one here except for you
has the greatest pleasure of being able to see me." I snorted at that. I
could see him, but it certainly wasn't a *pleasure* at all. That was when
realisation hit me like a bomb.

"So people think I'm talking to myself," I said disbelievingly.

"Well done for figuring that out by yourself!" Ako said with
sarcasm, a lot of sarcasm. A girl who was washing her hands started
to look at me anxiously, as if I was more than a little bit crazy. She
edged the slightest bit nearer to the door as if planning an escape. I
sighed impatiently and turned to look at Ako once more.

"Why are you here? Are you trying to get me killed again?" I
asked, raising my eyebrows. If the answer to my question was yes,
I was going to have to run for it, like the girl who was washing her
hands had just done. When Ako continued to look at me quizzically,
I rolled my eyes and gave an exaggerated sigh.

"The day when you fell out of the sky, and nearly got me run
over by a car?" I questioned. Then a look of understanding fell upon
Ako's face; it was my turn to feel smug for once. The smug feeling
crumbled away when Ako opened his big mouth and spoke.

"Your accident had absolutely nothing to do with me. It is not
my fault that you continually appear in the wrong places at the
wrong time. You would have been hit even if I hadn't appeared and
talked to you," Ako proclaimed, looking superior. I flared up at once.
I mean, who wouldn't?

"No, I wouldn't! Why do you think I'm not dead by now? Because—"

"You have an Erylenne watching over you. Every person has one, and they protect you from danger," Ako said surprisingly. Pfft, I'm not stubborn for nothing. It would take more than an "Erylenne" to make me back down on an argument. Even the queen probably couldn't do that.

"Then how come I was hit?" I asked. For once, I had Ako speechless. Even though I barely knew him, I could tell that this did not happen very often.

"There were circumstances that could not be prevented." Even though he was talking in fancy gobbledegook, I got the message. Something had happened that couldn't be stopped. I wasn't done with Ako yet.

"If you hadn't talked to me, I would have gone ahead and wouldn't have been hit," I said relentlessly, knowing that my arguing wasn't about to calm off yet.

"Fine! If you don't believe that even if I hadn't talked to you, you would have been killed, then watch this," Ako said with an expression close to anger. He drew up a screen with his fingers, and what looked like a projector appeared. I stared at this with my mouth dangling open.

On the screen, I saw myself walking away from the school, wearing the same clothes that I had worn when I was hit. I paused at the little alleyway that my mother had always told me not to go through and went through. I came out at the end and turned right to cross the road, and the same car that had hit me came roaring down the road; and, with screeching tyres, it hit me.

"How on earth did you just do that?" I asked in amazement. I was pretty sure that you couldn't buy that type of television in a normal shop, let alone make it come out of your fingertips. Even

China hadn't advanced to that stage. Seriously, I wanted to go live to wherever he was living.

"Whatever," He said, looking embarrassed. "Anyway, the point is, even if I hadn't talked to you, you would have still been hit. I'm not saying that it's a good thing you nearly died, but I am saying that it wasn't my fault," Ako said. I looked into his eyes, and even though I couldn't read his mind, I could see that he was telling the truth.

"Okay. You win. We seriously need to get going, or we'll be late for lesson. What do you have next?" I asked, glad that it wasn't as hard as I thought it would've been to back down on an argument.

"My timetable is exactly the same as yours," Ako said with a mischievous glint in his eyes. "We better get going."

*   *   *

"Okay. Why are you following me around? For the past week, everywhere I go, you follow. What is it with you?" I asked, utterly and truly fed up with seeing him wherever I went. It's gotten to the point where JJ and Tamara think that either Ako is madly in love with me or a crazy stalker, both of which, in their opinion, wasn't a good thing.

I didn't blame them to be honest. Every time I asked him, he would shrug the question off with a question of his own. This time, I was certainly not going to let him ask me a question without him answering mine.

"Well? Are you some type of stalker or something? That's what it looks like to me," I asked, planting my feet on either side of the sidewalk like my mother had done not so long ago.

"Don't you think a stalker wouldn't show himself to whoever was being followed?" Ako asked me, stopping when he was directly in front of me. I stepped back to make more space between us.

"Stop doing that!" I cried. Seriously, it was getting well annoying now. How many more questions would he ask me before he answered mine?

"Doing what?" He asked me, having the nerve to spread out his arms innocently as if he was being blamed for nothing. I could see in his eyes he knew exactly what I was talking about.

"Don't you think that it would get a little bit frustrating that whenever I ask a question, you always ask me another question that I always answer?" I asked, knowing my eyes were glinting with annoyance the way they always did when I was angry or frustrated.

Ako seemed to deflate before my eyes. It occurred to me how much Ako had changed since the first time I met him. He was all pompous and posh, and, now, he is just an average boy who I wouldn't look at twice if I saw him on the streets. Now that I think about it, this was probably part of his disguise as a normal teenage boy.

"Okay. I think it is time I told you the truth." Ako sighed, and looked as if he had aged thirty years. I would have felt sorry for him if I hadn't felt so frustrated. I motioned for him to go on as it looked, for a minute, like he wasn't going to say a word.

"I have been assigned to you by 'The Great Lord.' I am to be your guardian and protector," Ako said all of this in one great, tumbling breath—Hell's bells. What on earth is happening to this world! And why does this Great Lord thingie magigie think that I need protecting or guarding or whatever he thinks. That is exactly what I asked him. And guess what? He answered my question with one of his own. This is some seriously bad habit he has.

"Think about what has happened in the past few weeks. Don't you think you need a little bit of protecting?" Ako asked me, folding his arms.

"That wasn't my question! My question was why the Great Lord thinks I need protecting and what my life has to do with his," I cried, sick and tired of hearing his voice asking me questions. For once in my stupid life, Ako answered me straight.

"The Great Lord thinks you need protecting because people are looking for you," Ako said surprisingly. Seriously? About three weeks ago, I was told that I was a seer and that I could read people's minds. Now, I'm being told that people are hunting me down. What a great life I lead. It's *so* annoying that I can't read Ako's mind and answer my own questions for myself like I had gotten used to doing. Oh well. No one said life was fair.

"Why are they looking for me?" I asked, pushing my luck to the limit. I might as well try though. To my surprise, Ako answered readily as if he knew I was going to ask him that question one day or another.

"Their prophetess has recently died from a heart attack. They have become accustomed to having a prophetess to help them prepare for the future. Without their reader of the future, they find themselves vulnerable to what is yet to come. Their task of finding the Scroll of Elysium would be much harder without a prophetess," Ako said, avoiding answering my question fully—so much for answering "readily."

On the other hand, he had just told me what it was that the Tribe of Ironcia were looking for. To tell the truth, I knew that from the time I heard the names Tribe of Ironcia and Scroll of Elysium. I'm a genius if I do say so myself.

"Yes, but why do they want me? There must be other people in the world who can read the future, aren't there?" I asked, suddenly feeling unsure of myself. Ako took his time in answering my question.

"There are none that we know of. They have all died of heart attacks in one form or another. The privilege of being able to see through the veils of the future comes with consequences," Ako said in a low voice that I could barely hear.

I bet he was doing all he could for me to not know what he was talking about. What he didn't know was that there was no need for him to lower his voice as I already didn't understand what he was saying. It took a full minute for it to sink in that I would die earlier than the average human. Great, now I was getting a death sentence? How unfair can life get?

"Wait. Not all people who can read the future have died of heart attacks, have they?" I asked, desperately hoping that for once, the answer to my question would not leave me shaking. Obviously, my wish was no one's command.

"There is a chance that leaving your body behind and travelling with your soul into the future can take a toll on the human body and weaken the heart," Ako explained with a look of sympathy on his face. I hate it when people feel sorry for me. I could tell that Ako regretted telling me this little piece of info.

"Can I go now? I only need a little bit of time alone. You know, to think about what you just told me," I asked Ako cautiously. He merely nodded his head and walked me to my house. I let myself in through the front door and, without saying a word, closed the door behind me.

"Is that you, Beryl?" My mother's voice chirped, unnaturally sweet. What on god's green earth was going on here? My mother had started acting like a harpy when she usually acted like a banshee. It was really strange. On a normal day, my mum would be walking around the house making people's lives a misery, but, now, you would be more likely to find her bustling around, cleaning the house, and cooking dinner.

My brother walked down the stairs still wearing his school uniform and rolled his eyes when he saw me staring in shock at the newly decorated house. The porch was painted baby pink, and the hallway was a slighter deeper shade of pink. There were lacy curtains that were also, sadly, pink and were draped on the staircase.

"Get used to this. It looks like the rest of the house will soon be identical to this," Adrian told me. He was my older brother and the most annoying by far. He had weird hazel eyes that seemed to change colour in the sunlight and, with his olive skin, looked strange to me but cute to other people—bleurgh.

I walked up the stairs and into my room, and I flopped down onto my bed, throwing my rucksack down beside me. I took out my English book to finish off my essay on creative writing, and a piece of crumpled up paper dropped out of it. I smoothed it out, not really paying attention to what I was doing. I dimly registered in the back of my mind that the name of some sort of website was written clearly on the paper. I stared at it for about ten seconds before I realised what it was.

It was the website that Adira had thrown at my head while I was still in hospital. I felt a sort of tingly feeling in my fingers as I read and reread what was written there.

"Time to find out what it means," I said to myself. I practically ran to my computer and switched it on, thrumming my fingers impatiently against the mouse board. When it finally loaded up, I clicked on the internet as fast as I could and typed in the address. I was about to press enter when I heard a voice behind me.

"You were honestly going to do this without me?" Adira asked me, leaning casually on my wardrobe as if she had been there the whole time. Knowing now what life was really like, I guessed that she probably had been there the whole time. I screeched and nearly fell out of the chair as I jumped on my feet and whirled around.

"Beryl, is everything okay up there?" My mother's voice trilled. I took in a deep breath and answered back as normally as I could considering that I had just been on the verge of a heart attack. "Yeah, I'm good," I said, my voice shaking only slightly. I must not have been as good an actor as I thought I was as I heard a creaking noise coming from downstairs.

I saw this little video in my mind of my mother getting up from her usual seat in front of the telly to come up the stairs to check that everything was all right. In a blind panic, I grabbed Adira and threw her into the wardrobe that she had been leaning against so casually moments before. I leaped onto my bed and opened my English book at a random page. Seconds later, my mother opened the door with a fake smile plastered across her face.

"Is everything okay?" my mother asked me, her eyes narrow with suspicion.

"Yeah, everything's fine, Mum. Why?" I asked innocently, looking up at my mother as if I had just been reading. That was true at least. I *had* been reading—a computer screen.

"Oh well, nothing, dear. I just thought I heard some noise and thought my little popkin was in trouble," my mother said. She began walking around the room, looking through every gap or possible place to hide things.

"Uh, Mum? What are you doing?" I asked cautiously. I mean, my mother was acting as if she had been hit around the head with a frying pan recently.

"I'm just looking for the, um, the house phone," my mother said, not stopping to talk. She paused in front of the wardrobe with her arm stretched out. I quickly dived into my mother's mind and quickly told her as if she was the one thinking the thought that she had already looked in the cupboard. I quickly looked away from the back of my mother's head and at the wall.

"Mum, you just looked there." I complained in my whiniest voice. I hoped with all my heart that my mother would fall for it. My mother paused, clearly thinking hard. I didn't even have to read her mind to know that.

"Right you are, dearie. Well, I'll just look downstairs, shall I?" my mother said, clearly disgruntled that she hadn't found anything to punish me for. I held my breath until my mother waddled out of the room. I waited until my mum had creaked down the stairs.

"Whew! That was close." I half-grumbled half-whispered. When Adira didn't reply, I got slightly worried.

"Adira? Adira!" I got up and walked to the direction of the cupboard. I was about to open the door when I heard a muffled voice.

"A little help in here?" Adira's voice seeped through the wood of the wardrobe. I opened the door to see Adira sprawled on the floor of the cupboard, with clothes all over her body and face. Laughing, I helped her up and threw the clothes back into a messy heap, not caring in the slightest that my wardrobe looked as if an earthquake had hit it.

I sat down directly in front of the computer, and Adira dragged my old beanie next to me and made herself at home.

"What exactly *is* this website anyway?" I asked, watching Adira closely from the corner of my eyes to see how she would react to my question. Her face remained expressionless.

"You'll see soon enough," Adira said with her voice just as impassive as her facial expressions. Knowing that Adira wouldn't give me so much as a hint as to what the website was, I saved my breath and didn't ask her another question.

The computer had automatically switched off, and I had to type in all the details and passwords all over again. Jeez, I really should get around to telling my mother that we have *way* too many codes.

When I had finally finished typing in the codes and all the other bullpoopie needed to access the computer, I typed the website address into the Internet Explorer and waited for it to load up. If I haven't already told you before, my computer is, well, slow. Once it had finally loaded up, it was nothing compared to what I had expected it to be.

"You have got to be kidding me," I said in disbelief as a page full of what appeared to be children's nursery rhymes popped up on the screen. I looked at Adira who seemed enthralled at what had come up on the screen and looked completely ecstatic. I looked closer at the screen to try and find what Adira found so fascinating about a bunch of rhymes. I looked on the screen to find that they were songs about Aya. I looked at the first part, which seemed to be a sort of chant.

> All hail the saviour of the ancient tribes.
> All hail she who lived.
> In memory of the gifts she willingly gave,
> We all sing with pride and joy.
> All hail the saviour of the ancient tribes!

I scrolled down, amazed at the skill of the poetry that seemed to make the simply written words jump out of the screen and celebrate. The poems seemed to all be about how great and wise Aya was, and they didn't give the slightest hint that there was more than one person in the tribe.

"The poems change every time I go to the website," Adira said dreamily. "Last week, they were all about the war of the ancient tribes." I scrolled down lower, and I saw a poem that nearly made my poor heart stop beating. It was a poem—about me. It didn't say my name in the poem, but you could tell that it was about moi.

> She tries. She fails.
>
> She lives. She dies.
>
> Will she save our ancient tribe?
>
> Or leave us all to diminish and die?
>
> The choice rests upon her shoulders.
>
> Be our saviour once more, chosen.

I finished reading the poem before Adira did, and I looked at her without looking her in the eye with a great question mark on my face. She looked up at me with resolve in her eyes. Without thinking, I threw a mental barrier up in my mind, stopping me from sliding into hers. To my surprise, it worked. I stayed where normal people should stay: out of other people's minds.

I smiled, proud of finally being able to look people in the eye. I was getting tired of people thinking that I was a thief or a murderer because I didn't look them in the eye. For a second or two, I completely forgot about the prophecy and all of the other things that didn't add up to a normal person. I sat there with a huge silly grin on my face.

"Um, hello? Is anybody in there?" Adira asked, pretending to knock on the side of my head. "You were just asked to be the saviour of an ancient tribe, and you're just sitting there with a stupid grin on your face? Wow. I knew you were stupid but not *this* dumb."

My soppy grin slowly slid off my face, and it wasn't because of what Adira said. There was a little black arrow pointing downwards. I could tell from just one glance that this was no normal arrow that you would find in normal daily life. It felt like . . . like it—I could tell that Adira was thrown off track as well as she suddenly stopped talking, and that was no easy feat.

"This is not good," Adira murmured to herself.

"What's not good?" I couldn't stop myself from asking. Anyway, Adira was bound to ignore my question, just like she ignored everything else I said. To my surprise, she answered my question for once.

"This arrow is the sign of the dark arts. Anywhere you see that, it means that a dark caster is involved. If you have any sense, you would know the dark arts are involved and run for your life," Adira said darkly. I still didn't get why Adira had a look of worry that seemed to be permanently etched on her face.

"Yeah, but it's just a little drawing on a website. It doesn't mean that it's meant for me or anything," I said, shrugging my shoulders.

"You just don't get it, do you?" Adira asked me. When I merely shrugged my shoulders again, Adira looked as if she was silently restraining herself from having a fit. When she had calmed down enough to answer her own question, I quietly vowed not to do anything that would make her mad like that again.

"This website changes according to whoever goes onto it. For instance, if I logged on, it would be different from what you are now seeing. This website knows who is using it. This website knows that you are using it," Adira explained, clearly trying not to show how frustrated she was with me. I put two and two together, and I finally realised what Adira had been telling me. The website thingie magigie knew that I was on it. The arrow had appeared because they (whoever they were) knew I was logged on, and some dark caster had put it there.

There was only one thing left to do. I moved the mouse, and clicked on the arrow before Adira could say another word.

"Beryl! Have you completely lost your mind?" Adira half-shrieked. I turned my head automatically towards the door.

"Shut up! Are you *trying* to make my mother come up here and kill us?" I practically yelled in shock. I mean, she might be fine with dying, but I most certainly was not.

"She won't come. I've taken care of that," Adira muttered. She turned away from the computer screen and rubbed her temples as if she was thinking hard. I looked at the screen, curious as to what was going to happen next. The screen had gotten darker, until it was pitch black, the colour that you would expect to see at the dead of night.

I gasped out loud when words came sliding onto the screen one by one. They were the colour of blood. Adira turned around when she heard me gasp, and, once she had read what was on the screen, a moan escaped her. It was the prophecy written in the same curling, Edwardian script. I thought it was fine that this *magical* website knew about the prophecy, but clearly, judging from her reaction, Adira and I were of opposite minds. I was about to exit the web page when more words came sliding out from the side of the screen.

> *Roses are red.*
> *Violets are blue.*
> *We know what you are*
> *And where to find you.*

I stared at the screen in a state of total shock. I glanced over at Adira and saw that she had flung her arms over her face as if she was warding off a demon. It would have been comical if I didn't know what she was so scared of.

To my surprise, I wasn't scared at all. Yes, maybe I was surprised, but that seemed to be it. I looked at it logically. The poem *could* be from those people that Ako had told me about earlier on today. Crikey, I wouldn't want to be found by them. It would explain why the poem said *what* and not *you*. If they thought I was some kind of animal, they were going to get a pretty big shock if they came to find me.

I seriously hope that they weren't Dark casters or whatever Adira was saying. I glanced anxiously out of the window into the dark, checking to see that there weren't any flying evil things. Next to me, Adira opened her eyes; and, in them, I could read resolve. I had put up my mental barriers again, so I didn't read her mind as I was sure that Adira wouldn't appreciate that at all.

"We need to figure out what to do. You stupidly opened this page—"

"Uh, correct me if I'm wrong, but the page would still be there even if I hadn't opened it. All I did was read it, so we now have some type of warning as to what might happen to me," I retorted.

"Yes, but these people now know that you have read this page and that you know about them!" Adira shrieked. She had me there. Damn. If she was on the school debating society, they would be top of the league or whatever those people call it.

"There's no point in arguing about whether I did the right thing or not. What's done is done," I said in my most grown-up voice. Adira had the decency to look abashed, but it lasted for about a split second. Oh well. At least there was *something*.

"It might be from those people Ako was telling me about earlier on," I said, mostly to myself. Adira was on alert as soon as I mentioned Ako.

"Wait a minute . . . . Did Ako tell you about the tribe of Ironcia?" Adira asked me, disbelief rippling through her clear, brown eyes.

"If you're talking about those people whose prophetess died and are looking for me, then yes," I answered, surprised at the flash of anger that sparked up in her eyes. I couldn't resist the temptation to read her mind any longer. I threw down the mental barriers and looked deep into her eyes.

In her mind, I could see that there was a small white door that said the words "Enter." I took it as an invitation for me to walk straight through the door and find out what the hell was happening in there. Hell's bells—there were two people deep in conversation who I would call normal looking except that they were abnormally tall, and they had great wings folded against their backs.

One of the bird men had wings that were of a colour so white and so pure that it would make fresh snow look yellow compared to it. I'm not even exaggerating. The other bird man had powerful-looking grey wings that were flecked here and there with black. Wild guess, but I don't think they're part of the tribe of Ironcia. For one thing, I certainly don't have any wings.

"Why do you have this strange inclination to protect this human girl, my lord? I understand that she is gifted with powers beyond the ordinary, but I still do not comprehend why she needs our protection." The grey winged man was saying in a deep, powerful voice. I took it that they were talking about me.

"It is not a matter of wanting, Jodreus." The white-winged man said majestically in a voice that would expect a king to use. Come to think of it, if the grey winged man was calling him master, he was probably their leader.

I waited for him to say more, but he stayed quiet. I heard a slight coughing to my right, and I noticed Adira for the first time. Everything clicked together. The two bird men haven't noticed me because *I was in a memory!* Adira was sitting on an intricately patterned gold stool that appeared to have little wings coming out from the legs. She was scribbling on what appeared to be parchment.

"My lord, forgive me, but I do not understand what you are saying," Jodreus said, a look of slight confusion showing in his large, brown eyes.

"I take it that you know by now that a prophecy was made earlier on this year. The prophecy foretold that the Scroll of Elysium would be taken again. The choice rests solely on the girl who could just as easily save our lives as she could destroy it," the one with white wings explained.

"I still do not fully understand you. How will what goes on in the lives of humans affect our lives?" Jodreus asked. I could see that the Lord or whatever his name is was getting impatient.

"Don't you understand? The Scroll of Elysium contains all of the love, happiness, and luxury. We may be living in the heavens above, but we are too close to being safe from its wrath. In addition to that, most of our wives are mortal, and if they were to see their descendants living a life of pain, they would most certainly turn against us for not preventing this from happening," the one with white wings said passionately, his bare chest heaving. A look of enlightenment was dawning in Jodreus's face. Seriously, how dumb can you get?

"We must send down a man from our troops to protect and oversee the life of this girl, my lord. But he mustn't tell the girl of what we are doing," Jodreus said, gathering up the books and papers that were strewn across the table and the floor in some cases. Jeez, they were awfully messy for a couple of winged guys. They both stood up and walked out of the room together still talking about the best way to protect moi, leaving Adira still scribbling feverishly on the piece of parchment like there would be no tomorrow. As the door closed behind the bird men, I felt myself being sucked back into reality.

I plonked down onto my bed as soon as my feet touched the floor of my bedroom. I stared at Adira dumbstruck, seeing her in a completely new light. Even though this memory or whatever it was didn't have much to do with my question, I was glad to have seen it. She merely looked down at her hands and twiddled her thumbs around each other.

"Who are you?" I asked in a flat voice that sounded nothing like the usual me. JJ would have had a heart attack if she ever heard me talk like that in front of her. Adira took longer than I thought she would to answer my question, probably thinking whether to tell me the truth.

It occurred to me that I didn't know anything really about Adira. Yeah, I know her name, but that's pretty much it. I don't even know her *surname*.

"I am the royal scribe to the Wrayalis. Every person that I could call family had already died when I was fifteen years old from the Bubonic Plague. I survived, but I was afraid to die, so I joined the Wrayalis through meditation day and night for the next seven years, surviving on only water," Adira said slowly, as if something she didn't want me to know would suddenly jump out from her mouth.

I stared at her with my mouth agape like a door with loose hinges. I looked at her disbelievingly, but when I looked her in the eyes (mental barriers up), all I could read there was honesty. Wow. The girl sitting in front of me was nearly seven hundred years old if my maths was correct (It probably wasn't.). That was a world record broken. I couldn't help it, but my insides were squirming with smugness. Finally, I was getting the truth!

"Is Ako part of the Wrayalis as well?" I asked her, my voice a little less hostile than it had been before.

"Yes, he was chosen to come and protect you and to oversee the choices you have to make," Adira said all of this very quickly as if she somehow hoped I wouldn't be able to hear or understand what she was saying if she said it all faster. Like that's going to work. I talk really fast, and, practically, no one understands me half the time.

"Why couldn't you tell me any of this before?" I questioned. This was beginning to sound like *Who Wants to Be a Millionaire*.

"The Great Lord thought it wouldn't be wise to alarm you and cause unnecessary stress," Adira replied, looking me straight in the eye. I made my mental barriers stronger so I could focus on asking the questions instead of trying not to read her mind. I ploughed on through my questions, and Adira answered them truthfully (I think), but she was getting oddly more and more formal.

I didn't stop until I was sure that I knew every single thing about her. I could have just read her mind and answered my own questions for myself, but I wanted to hear those words coming out from her mouth instead of forcing it from her without giving her a choice.

"Do you think you're going to be done with asking me questions anytime soon? I need to go soon. Make that now," Adira said, staging a loud, obviously-fake yawn. I would bet a whole bank full of money that Adira was pretty much completely annoyed with me.

I don't see why she's not more than happy that I didn't try and kill her or anything drastic like that. My annoyance with her didn't make me feel any less hurt when Adira tossed her braided hair over a slender shoulder and sauntered out of the room.

I continued staring at the door long after Adira left. I was in my own little world of daydreaming. Even if Adira didn't want to tell me anything about her, I had forced it out of her. Wow. Adira was over seven hundred years old, she didn't eat food for seven years straight, and she was the royal scribe to a legendary species. Huh, that explained Adira's strange love of writing. I collapsed on my bed, my mind full to bursting point with stuff that a normal sane person wouldn't believe. My eyes drifted shut of their own accord. I was 100% sure that no one could have had a stranger day than me.

CHAPTER 4

For the first time in the history of my magnificent life, I woke up on time for school and managed to have a decent, long shower instead of the mad rush that usually awaits me every morning. I could smell the scent of food while I was putting my clothes on, and my ravenous stomach growled at me. I could almost hear it yelling at me to go get some food. I yanked my boots on and walked out of my bedroom quite calmly compared to how I usually walk (make that run) on a normal school day.

"Beryl! It's time to wake up, dearie!" my mother yelled up the stairs while bustling around the kitchen making omelette and beans for breakfast judging from the smell that was wafting around the house. It occurred to me that my mother had changed a lot over the past few weeks. For one thing, she wasn't the evil old hag that she used to be, but she was now the proper mother that I had always longed for. Now that my wish had come true, I felt nothing but uncomfortable.

My mother probably started being nice to me because she probably felt bad about my father kicking the bucket and felt that if she was a better mother, we wouldn't be as sad. Pfft, like that was going to work.

I wasn't actually feeling sad at all about my father croaking, and I'm pretty much sure Adrian and Carla (my little sister) weren't feeling too sad about my dad. I mean no offense, but my father wasn't the greatest. I mean, Carla hasn't seen him since she was like two years old. I walked into the kitchen, and my mother was so surprised to see me that she actually stopped cooking for about five seconds.

"What a nice surprise to see you awake for once!" my mother said in a falsely cheerful voice, even though her eyes looked hollow and full of despair. I couldn't resist finding out what had made her so upset. I looked straight into her eyes, all mental barriers gone, and indulged myself in her thoughts.

Crap. It was exactly what I was thinking; make that what she was thinking about. My mother was thinking about my father and if she had made the right choice in signing a divorce with him. I felt like yelling at my mother and telling her not to be such a wallower (if that was even a word). Jeesh, some adults never learn, do they?

I looked away from my mother and put up the mental barriers again, trying to be, for once, a normal teenage girl. I grabbed the plate of buttered toast and tried not to look as if I had been where normal people shouldn't be able to go.

"Darling, why don't you have some omelette? They're freshly cooked!" my mum said in a forced, cheerio voice. It was actually quite funny watching my mother try to act happy when, in reality, she was burning inside. I felt a fierce rush of affection for my mother, and this was so surprising that I nearly dropped my plate of toast.

I mean, come on. Give the woman some slack. Her husband had died less than a month ago, and she was trying to be a good mother for our sake. I must have been completely out of my mind as I leaned on to my mother and hugged her softly, breathing in her own unique scent. If JJ or Tamara had been with me, they would have called the mental hospital straight away, no doubt about that.

"I'm not hungry, but I better get to school now. I've got an appointment with my English teacher," I said in my normal speaking voice. Technically, I did have one, but, on the other hand, Ms. Sparks didn't know that she had an appointment. Oh well, details don't matter in my world.

I grabbed a slice of jammy toast and walked out of the door before my mother could ask me what the hell I was doing. To be honest, I would have had no answer to that question. I had just reached the end of the road when—guess what? It started pouring rain. I was about to start running to school when I heard a voice behind me, calling my name. Crap. It sounded just like—

"Beryl? What are you doing out here so early? Are you on steroids or something?" Ako asked me, raising his dark eyebrows. God, why do I have to get the worst life?

"I'm going to school, and don't worry, I'm not going to drop dead from a heart attack anytime soon. I'll let you know if I feel like dying," I said sardonically, not caring too much that it wasn't his fault that my heart would stop beating from shock. It was too bad for him that he had been the one to tell me that little piece of info.

"You know perfectly well that you having a heart attack has nothing to do with me. I just happened to be the unfortunate person to tell you," Ako retaliated, his pretty boy eyes flashing with annoyance. Unable to think of anything else to say to him without being downright untruthful, I merely huffed at him and lengthened my stride. Seeing as Ako was a lot taller than I was, it made no difference.

"Look, I'm sorry that you are going to one day die of shock, but you have to know that it's not my fault," Ako said, holding my elbow and making me look him in the eye. I panicked, completely forgetting that I couldn't read Wrayalis' minds. I floundered in the rain for about ten seconds before I realised that I couldn't read Ako's damn mind. I honestly think I should go into therapy. Friggin' crazy, that's what I am.

I looked at Ako, and I saw such sincere honesty that I couldn't help but feel guilty. Sadly, I wasn't feeling guilty enough to apologise to him.

"Okay." Ako's face broke out into a smile with that single word. "But I seriously need to know more about these tribal people if they are going to hunt me down."

"Well, the tribe of Ironcia is said to have been formed before the time of even Christ," Ako began, letting go of my arm and beginning to walk again. "They were chosen for their strength, speed, and agility. Most important of all, they were chosen for the quality of their gifts." Ako paused to take in a breath. I took this as an opportunity to do my most favourite thing in the world—talking.

"Were all of the people who were in this *tribe* related to Aya?" I asked, turning my head to look at Ako.

"No, by the gods, they weren't. This was before the War of Crivial," Ako explained. He gave me a knowing look that probably meant that he already knew that I knew about the war of Crivial. He might as well be psychic for god's sake. For all I knew, he probably knew Adira. It would actually make sense if he did as he supposedly was part of the Wrayalis. Thinking about it didn't exactly help.

"Wait, you don't happen to know Adira, do you?" I asked warily, stopping midstride but having to continue walking when Ako showed no signs of slowing down. He was smiling slightly. He tapped his nose when he caught me looking at him.

"Well?"

"No can do." Ako said with a childish look on his face like that of a little boy who had been caught stealing sweets by his mother. There was really no point in saying that; if he hadn't known, he would have been like "*who?*" So it was fairly obvious that he knew who the hell I was talking about. I harrumphed and continued walking as if I was oblivious to what Ako was trying to say—I wish.

We turned to a corner into a road that was one street away from the school, and, god forbid, I wish I was already there in a warm classroom instead of being drenched in the rain. We walked in a companionable silence until I had to have the mother of all yawns and shiver violently like I had just been electrified.

"Aren't you going to tell me more about these tribal people?" I asked reluctantly, not wanting to be the person to break the silence. I glanced over at Ako to find him looking perfectly comfortable with rain beating us up. He unwillingly looked up at me.

"What do you want to know?" he asked me. Does he have memory loss or something because it was seriously beginning to get on my nerves, the casual way he forgot things.

"What you were just saying, not five minutes ago," I said with suppressed politeness. I can tell you now, it was not easy. Ako grunted with obvious discomfort.

"As the years passed, the members began to argue. At first, it was minor arguments that you would expect to find in even the happiest household in the world." I snorted at that. "Gradually, they evolved into bigger fights that nearly killed the leader. The tribe separated, and it was thought that they would never join as one again. They became arch enemies. They fought for land, power, and basically everything.

A part of the tribe gave up their fighting ways and settled down to live on a large, spacious piece of land that was well suited for living. They had many children and grandchildren and thus lived happily and in harmony.

Sadly enough, the other half of the tribe were angry that they had been deserted by their own leader. That was the way they saw it. They fought long and hard with the elders who were the people who first came to the land, not physically but verbally.

Eventually, a war was started. It was called the War of the Tribes. The good tribe, as you would call it, lost heavily, and many people were killed. There was only one survivor. You may know of her. Her name was—"

"Aya!" I blurted out, unable to help myself. I mean, come on, I was proud to finally know something.

"You know about her?" Ako asked me, looking impressed. Finally, I get a little gratitude for knowing something. I tried hard not to look too pleased with myself.

"Uh, yeah, she's the one who had those powers."

"Anyway, she was the only person who survived. That is the story of the tribe," Ako finished off somewhat lamely.

"I don't get it. These tribal stories have to be from millions of years ago. What does it have to do with me?" I asked Ako, sure that he wouldn't have an answer to my question. Sadly, as know it all's go, he had an answer ready as if he knew I would ask him this question.

"I am sure you know all about spirits and such," Ako said. We had now reached the school gates, but I wasn't about to let him escape without me knowing everything that I wanted to know.

"Yeah, but they're obviously not real." I laughed. I wasn't about to tell him that I had been visited by my dead father while I was in hospital. That would probably just make me act like a banshee. I haven't told anybody, and I don't plan to.

"They are as real and true as definitely as I am standing here in front of you," Ako proclaimed grandly as if he was announcing the Olympic winners.

"Oh!" I cried, throwing my arms out as if I was so surprised at what he was saying. Judging by the look of shock on Ako's face, I had gone overboard on the acting. Oh well. Now, I know what to watch out for if I ever want to go into an acting career.

He blinked his eyes and carried on talking as if nothing had happened. "Yeah, well, the leader of the attacking group has come back as a person. The Great Lord suspects that he is controlling a human, and, once he has done what he needs to do, he will simply posses him and live once again as a person," Ako explained simply. Wow. This leader person sure will have a heck of a time.

"Wait a sec." I stopped Ako from going to his class or wherever he was thinking of going to. "What does he want to do?"

"To make you part of what he calls his tribe. Once he has done that, he will attempt to steal the Scroll of Elysium," Ako said, backing away from me and walking in through the school gates. How rude.

"How do you know all this?" I yelled after him, making sure that he wouldn't be able to fake not hearing me. He spun around like a man version of a ballerina, and, grinning, he tapped his nose twice—men.

I walked into the school playground sick and tired of being blanked by people when I most needed them, pfft. I sat down comfortably under the shade of the trees, wringing my hair out. The courtyard was still empty, and, to be honest, I wasn't really surprised. I mean, most people come running into school when the second bell is ringing. Hell, I was one of those people.

I glanced up at the window of Ms. Sparks's office and saw the curtains were drawn, and a fresh vase of flowers stood on the windowsill. I sighed. It's time to go and face my fears. In other words, I had to go and tell Ms. Sparks what happened yesterday.

I stood up warily and stretched out my legs. I practically ran to the entrance, half-drowning from the pounding rain that just would not stop! Why do I have to be the freaky psychic and mind reader? I'd rather be a witch so I can stop this freaking rain.

Once I entered the muffled silence of the school, I slowed down and squeaked my way to Ms. Sparks's office. I paused in front of her office door, and, not wanting to be rude, I knocked smartly three times on the large wooden door that looked as though it had come from the middle ages. I pulled my mental barriers closer to me and made them stronger than they already were.

"Come in," Ms. Sparks's sharp voice said. At least, I assumed it was her. I pushed open the door slowly and walked into the room, surprised at how normal her office looked. I mean, I was expecting her to have erected shrouds at the very least.

"Oh hello, Beryl," Ms. Sparks beamed, her voice warming when she recognised me. I was surprised to see her usually stern face split into a wide smile that was scary to see. Her eyes looked unusually bright.

"Are you feeling okay Ms. Sparks?" I asked cautiously, my hand resting lightly on the doorknob.

"I am fine, fine, no need to worry. It is just that my mother passed away yesterday," Ms. Sparks said, flushing slightly as she said it like a little girl who'd gotten an award from the head teacher.

I stared at her in shock like she was crazy. What type of person would be happy to see their mother dead unless she was a horrible old hag? Even then, it still wouldn't be normal not to feel a little bit of remorse. If they were crazy, that'd be an all right excuse, but Ms. Sparks was clearly sane (I hope), and she seemed happy enough.

I mouthed wordlessly like a goldfish and tried to open the door from behind, but, sure enough, it was locked. Great, I was in a locked room with a psycho who would probably kill me.

"Beryl," Ms. Sparks said softly. I turned around to see Ms. Sparks still sitting in her plump leather chair, the flush receding from her cheeks.

"Yes?" I asked shakily, my voice sounding as if it hadn't been in use for quite a bit of time. I cleared my throat nervously.

"I'm sorry. That didn't come out as I would have like to have said it. What I meant to say is that what you people call death has happened to my mother," Ms. Sparks explained, speaking in riddles. She was still basically telling me that her mama had died, just in other words. My face must have told her that I didn't understand what she was trying to say to me as she hurried on in her explanation.

"When a magically gifted person dies, they do not go where all of the deceased people go. They live on in a special place that is unknown to the living. My mother struggled with life in pain, and she was put out of her misery yesterday. I cannot help but feel happy for her," Ms. Sparks explained, her voice trembling slightly.

In some weird way, I understood what she was trying to say. I still didn't understand why she would be so happy that she would announce it to me as if she had won a grand prize. She was probably just hysterical. Why do so many people have to die? First, my father; and, now, Ms. Sparks's mum. Even though Ms. Sparks was like a century older than me, I still felt quite sorry for her. Before I could feel too sorry for her, Ms. Sparks switched back into strict-high-school-teacher mode.

"Okay then Beryl, enough chit chat about my family life," Ms. Sparks said briskly. Her sharp tone was softened when she gave me a small smile. "What did you want to tell or ask me?"

"Well, I . . . uh, I've got my English essay," I mumbled lamely, holding it out to her. She gave me "The Look" that all adults have and use a lot of the time. She took it from my hand gingerly as if it might be infected with some horrible disease and put it down on the side of her desk. She looked at me with knowing eyes.

"Is there anything else?" Ms. Sparks asked me. I stared at her. It was almost as if she knew what I was going to say. I swear, if the real Ms. Sparks had been kidnapped by aliens and left the person in front of me behind, I wouldn't be surprised.

"Well, yeah," I said, suddenly unsure whether I should tell her or not. "Yesterday, I was on the computer, and—"

"Beryl, please don't tell me that you went on that damned abnormal website," Ms. Sparks said, her pale cheeks flushing.

"Well, yeah," I repeated, not sure what else to say. "But how did you know?" I asked, watching as Ms. Sparks stood up and began pacing the room while muttering under her breath. She completely ignored my question, and I was sure that if I suddenly gave birth to a litter of monkeys, she would continue to ignore me.

To be honest, it was really strange watching a grown woman walk around the room talking to herself. She appeared to be having a full blown conversation with herself, and I only caught snatches of what she was saying. I was sure I heard my name mentioned and something that sounded a lot like an arrow. I dozed off into dreamland, imagining I was on a beach in Hawaii.

"It can't be," she said suddenly in a normal voice. I jumped when I heard her voice. She had, after all, been muttering nonstop under her breath like a raving lunatic.

"What was that you just said?" I questioned indifferently like I had been listening to everything she had been saying. As if.

"Never mind that. Did you hear what I just asked you?" she asked me impatiently, her moss green eyes bulging slightly. I was almost too scared to reply.

"Sorry. No," I said shortly. Before I could say another word, she barrelled on in her police investigation.

"Did you happen to see a little black arrow at the bottom of the screen?" she asked me, looking slightly calmer than she did before. I fumbled for a second, not sure if I should tell her or not. I was scared that she would have a fit and lose her mind completely as well as her mother in the same day.

"Yes." To my surprise, Ms. Sparks didn't start spazzing out like I thought she would. Instead, she collapsed on her chair like an old man whose family had just been killed.

"You didn't happen to click on it, did you?" she asked me, closing her eyes as she spoke. She seemed to already know the answer, but it seemed that she wanted me to certify it.

"Yes," I whispered, suddenly ashamed of myself. Why on earth did I press the arrow? I might as well be retarded; it would make no difference to the way I acted. Ms. Sparks let out a long, drawn out sigh and opened her eyes slowly as if she had the weight of the whole world on her shoulders.

"And why, pray, did you press it?" Ms. Sparks inquired. Her voice had lost the hopelessness and now merely sounded curious.

"Well, I didn't know that the arrow thing was a bad thing or anything, and I didn't really think anything would happen if I pressed it." I sounded like a whiny kid who was trying to get out of trouble.

"What happened?" Ms. Sparks asked me. She was seriously freaking me out. A second ago, she was all mad and hysterical;

and, now, she was the calm, down to earth Ms. Sparks that I knew. Thank god for that, but it was still kind of freaky.

"Well, when I pressed the arrow thing, the screen went all dark, and then the prophecy came sliding out from the side of the screen in the colour of blood." I stopped, unsure whether I should carry on. Ms. Sparks nodded like she wanted me to carry on talking.

"Once the prophecy had come out on the screen, I was going to exit the page, but then more words came out." I paused again, but, this time, to look at Ms. Sparks's expression. Her face was blank, as if she was listening to no more than a children's story.

I continued, not knowing if she was even listening to me. "There was some sort of poem written under there. It started off with that beginning thing that most poems have. It was something like '*Roses are red, violets are blue; we know what you are and where to find you,*'" I recited, chancing a glance at Ms. Sparks. I was about to tighten my mental barriers when I realised that Ms. Sparks was closing her eyes, and I couldn't read people's minds without looking them straight in the eyes. That seriously sucks. Ms. Sparks opened her eyes, and I had to quickly avert my gaze before she could be even more pissed than she already was.

"Beryl, it is as I feared. I assume Ako has already explained to you about the tribe of Ironcia, hasn't he?" Ms. Sparks asked me, raising her head a little higher. It gave me a chance to study her without reading her mind. She looked pale and drawn out as if the Scroll of Elysium had already been stolen and used. Her skin looked greyer than it had been when I had first gone inside her office, and she looked about ten years older.

Jeez, it was about time she went on one of those sixty-minute makeover shows. It would seriously help her. I realised that I had been gawking at her like an idiot for about a minute, and I still hadn't answered her question.

"Yeah, they're the people who want me to read the future for them or whatever it is they want me for." I shrugged, knowing from the look of approval on Ms. Sparks's face that I was right.

"Yes, that is exactly right. They want to use your skills to their advantage and to help them find the Scroll of Elysium." I waited for her to say something, but she kept silent. I looked into her eyes, strengthening my mental barriers so hard that I felt I would lose my mind. I'm not even joking. To my surprise, I could see hesitation in them clearly.

Curious, I began to lower my mental barriers, but I stopped short, remembering how much Ms. Sparks hated me reading her mind. I didn't really blame her to be honest. I mean, if some little kid kept butting into the privacy of my mind, I'd probably throw them out of the window. Instead, I waited patiently the way a normal human would, and I waited for her to speak.

"The leader of the natural tribe has come back in spirit form, and he currently possesses the body of a deceased person." Eww, that is way gross. That wasn't like oh-my-god news though (for a normal person maybe, but not for me), so I didn't really get why Ms. Sparks didn't want to tell me. She should have known by now that I wasn't the squeamish type of girl who threw up at the very mention of blood.

I looked over at Ms. Encyclopaedia and saw that she was holding something back. Don't ask me how I knew, but, somehow, I did. She looked like she was arguing with herself, and I swear I could hear her whispering to some person. This woman is seriously going bonkers.

"Ms. Sparks? Are you feeling okay?" I looked at her anxiously while crossing my fingers and praying fervently that Ms. Sparks hadn't gone completely la-la.

"Me? Oh yes, I am completely fine," She said hurriedly, before resuming her conversation with what I assumed to be a ghost. I waited for about two minutes before clearing my throat. I wasn't trying to be smart or anything, but I had been listening to a one-sided conversation for what felt like hours.

"Oh, sorry, dear," Ms. Sparks said haphazardly. "I didn't realise that you were still here."

"Um, miss, I'm the only person in this room," I said, surprised that it was possible to go crazy in less than ten minutes. It's probably a world record broken.

"Ms. Sparks, who are you *talking* to?" I asked incredulously. She seemed to have all of her attention concentrated on me, and I felt her consciousness graze my barriers, willing them to break down.

I suddenly felt tired, the way an old man would feel after a long day at work. I let down the barriers and looked at a spot about one foot on top of Ms. Sparks's head. It was only when I was looking at the wall that I realised how much energy putting up mental barriers in my mind took. It felt like a heavy weight had been taken from me. I heard Ms. Sparks's voice calling me back down to earth, and I wearily focused on what she was saying.

"I am talking to my Inlai. Every person has one in them." Ms. Sparks tried to get me to look her in the eye, clearly forgetting that I was a mind reader. I stared resolutely at the ceiling even while I was talking to her.

"What exactly *is* an Inlai?" I asked, my face a total question mark. Ms. Sparks looked a lot happier at the change of subject. I'd never heard of an Inlai in my whole life; but, from what I know so far, they can argue with you, judging from the way Ms. Sparks had been speaking to whatever she thought she was talking to. I wouldn't be surprised if there was a human living inside of Ms. Sparks. After all, anything's possible.

"An Inlai is a part of the soul that has its own mind and characteristics. They have no form, and they are a part of you. Every whole human has an Inlai, but if the person does not know of them, their Inlai will keep quiet and take refuge with the soul until, eventually, the soul accepts the Inlai and forges them together as one," Ms. Sparks surprisingly explained.

I was about to be like "what are you talking about, you mad old hag," when I felt something within me stir. I opted for something less rude and more polite.

"Um, Ms. Sparks, I don't think I have one," I said. Well, I tried to say it, but, before I could get past the first words, Ms Sparks held up her hand like a Roman emperor for silence.

"As I said before, every person has an Inlai. Look deep within you, and find the most important part of the human nature. They only speak to you in moments of emergencies, but my Inlai is rather special, and I can speak to it anytime I wish to." She looked smug to be honest. Huh. Some type of teacher she is.

Not wanting to be downright ignorant, I closed my eyes and searched with my mind, yelling the word Inlai repeatedly. I mean, I didn't know its name; so what else was I supposed to call it?

"All right, all right, no need to yell," a sleepy voice that I had never heard before in my life grumbled. I gave a little shriek and looked at Ms. Sparks, checking that it wasn't her who had spoken. She was sitting as if nothing major had happened, and she was merely stuck in traffic. I took a deep breath in and closed my eyes for concentration.

"Okay. Who are you?" I asked whoever had spoken, hoping to god that I hadn't just gone mad and hearing mad.

"God, aren't you listening to anything that woman was saying? I am an Inlai," the voice said again. Great, I had a snob living inside me. I could tell from the voice that it was a girl speaking.

"Yeah, I figured that out. Thanks so much. What I'm trying to ask is what your name is," I asked, trying to be polite. I'd heard her speak barely two sentences, and I was already trying my hardest not to instantly hate her.

"My name is Birdie," Birdie said slowly and carefully as if she was talking to a two-year-old. I snorted at that. I mean, what type of a parent would name their daughter Birdie? A mentally ill mother, that's the answer.

I waited for Birdie to say something, but I heard a breathy snore, which probably meant that she was asleep—again. I opened my eyes to see Ms. Sparks looking at something on my chest. I looked down at the gold necklace that I had found this morning.

"Where did you get that locket?" Oh, so that was what she was looking at. I was beginning to wonder about her.

"Oh, I found it in my jeans this morning, but I couldn't get it to open. Why?" I stared at Ms. Sparks as she gazed at the necklace like the world had ended. I looked down but I couldn't find anything wrong with it.

"Look at it closely." I picked up the locket and held it up. Oh my god. There was that same little arrow engraved on the gold locket that was on the website. In other words, it was the sign of the Dark Arts. Wow. I felt like I was being stalked. In this case, I was being followed by something much worse than a murderer or a rapist. I yanked the locket off from my neck and dropped it onto the table where it lay quivering.

"How did you get it?" Ms. Sparks asked me again. This time, I thought harder than I had done before. I came up with a blank again. To be honest, I didn't even remember putting it on.

I'm really sorry, but I have no idea where it came from," I said, feeling quite scared that some person was following me without me even realising it. Either they were really good at hiding, or I was half-blind.

"From now on, I need you to be on the lookout for anything that may seem strange. If you see anything that you wouldn't normally see or if you see this arrow again, come straight to me and tell me. Have you seen anything odd in the past few weeks?" Ms. Sparks asked me, all traces of humour gone.

It was quite frightening to see how much Ms. Sparks feared and loathed the Dark Arts. My mother popped into my head. If anyone was acting strangely, it was my mother; but, somehow, I could tell that my mother wasn't exactly what Ms. Sparks was looking for.

"No, not really, I'll try and see if anything weird is happening though," I said in a reassuring voice. I hope. I still didn't understand why an arrow was enough for me to feel like I was in hell, but I wasn't about to ask. I glanced at the clock, and I saw that the bell was going to ring in about two minutes. I hurried on to my last question.

"Wait, whose body is the spirit thing using?" I asked, half-rising from my seat and grabbing my bag. It wasn't like I hadn't noticed Ms. Sparks avoiding having to answer my question. I sat back down comfortably, knowing that Ms. Sparks would make a huge scene. I was right. I waited for about what felt like a week, although logically, no more than five minutes could have gone by. I was almost certain that Ms. Sparks was talking to her Inlai again.

Finally, Ms. Sparks opened her mouth. I leaned in close, feeling dread lapping at my feet. A part of me felt like blocking my ears and running from the room, but curiosity made me stay rooted firmly in my seat. I got the weirdest feeling that it was someone I knew. But it couldn't be, because no one I knew had died, except for—

"It's your father's body, Beryl, dear, that he is using," Ms. Sparks whispered. I stared at a spot on the wall above her head in shock. I couldn't bring myself to think of my father's body being used like that—so much for RIP.

At first, all I could feel was disgust. I couldn't even begin to imagine my father's dead body, half-rotted away and alive but with a different mind. Gross. I looked at Ms. Sparks's forehead and waited for her to say something. Her forehead was creased up with worry lines, and her mouth was pursed like she was waiting for me in a bombshell of tears. Like that would ever happen.

"Ms. Sparks? Why is he using my father's body out of all the, um, corpses?" She opened her mouth and closed it again. She opened it once more, and I could tell that she was about to speak, when— guess what? The stupid bell rang. We both jumped, and I had to clap my hand over my mouth to muffle my shriek.

"Come on now, Beryl, you had better get to class now. I wouldn't want to be the reason for you to be late for class," Ms. Sparks said softly, giving me a feeling of calmness. The illusion was ruined when she gave a hysterical giggle. She bustled over to the door and opened it, leaving me no choice but to walk out and join the swarm of teenagers running to class. I paid no attention to where I was going, and I walked the direction of my locker, even though I was nearly ten minutes late for class.

Jeez, I might as well be blind. I leaned against the wall and took a deep breath in, then out, in, then out. I repeated this exercise until I was almost lightheaded from excess air.

My mind was still reeling from the shock of being told that my dead father's body was still in use. It did make sense though, in some freakishly weird way. If I didn't know about my father dying, I would have gone straight to the leader of the tribe without any questions, thinking that the spirit thing was my real father and not some dead corpse. In spite of everything they had done for me, I couldn't help but feel impressed by the way the tribe was thinking.

"Beryl?" For the second time this morning, Ako turned up in the most random places where I just happened to be. My hold on my sanity was broken into little pieces as I unleashed my anger on Ako. You couldn't really blame me for letting out all my frustration on him. Boy, did I feel sorry for him.

"You knew about my father, didn't you?" I asked in a low, serious voice that I had only used once in my life, and that was when my little sister had nearly set fire to my bedroom carpet using the candle lighter.

"Well, yeah," Ako said sheepishly, suddenly finding his shoes more interesting to look at than my face. If anything, that made me even madder. I'm the only person who has an excuse not to look people in the eye. Anyone else who doesn't look people in the eye is a plain old liar.

"And why didn't you tell me!" I yelled, not caring that we were in the middle of a school corridor where people were studying quietly. All I could think about was the anger that was blazing through my body, almost setting me alight. I would have missed Ako muttering a word hastily when I began yelling if my ears didn't suddenly turn super sensitive.

"Well, the Great Lord didn't—"

"Oh, well, he can go and just boil his head! On second thought, you're free to do so as well!" I screeched relishing in Ako's hurt. I didn't really care that soon, only dogs would be able to hear my yells. Ako opened his mouth to say something, but he closed his mouth as if he had thought better about what he was going to say. Good. If it was anything against me, I'd probably start a war against him and no bets as to who would win.

"You're not going to tell me anything else, are you?" I said in a voice that was a whisper compared to my shrieks. When Ako said nothing and merely looked down, I was back to the hating girl. "You know what I think of you? I think you're a little lapdog who worships the ground that the Great Lord steps on, and you can't think for yourself! Go back to wherever you came from, and stay there!"

I gave him one last look of disgust and flounced off the long way to my class, not wanting to have to walk past Ako. I was really mad, but I wasn't mad enough to skip class. When I turned around at the staircase, I could see that Ako was shaking his head dejectedly and looked like he had just gambled his life away. It was enough to make anyone's heart ache. My heart sure was aching, but it was from all the yelling I had done.

I marched to class with my head held high and my fists shaking with suppressed anger. It was enough to make any person run away screaming at the sight of me. I opened the door to my English class, praying that Ako wasn't sitting there like he usually did. To my surprise, the seat next to mine was empty. I walked to my seat and sat down, not bothering to tell the teacher why I was so late for class. Then I burst into big bawling baby's tears.

*　　*　　*

I was lying down on the couch in the living room flicking through the channels, not really taking in what I was seeing. I sighed. How come all the worst things seem to happen to me? I might as well commit suicide now and avoid living my stupid life. Why can't I have a heart attack now? Sadly, as life goes, you don't die when you want, but you die when you're most happy.

JJ and Tamara had already been here to see me earlier on in the afternoon, and it wasn't to make me feel better. It was to ask why I had been crying. Naturally, I wasn't feeling the greatest of all people and had yelled at them too, saying they were lousy friends and that I wished they had never been born. They'd walked out on me saying that when I calmed down and wasn't feeling so horrible and mean, they would consider talking to me again. I sort of deflated then and started crying again. My life seriously has turned upside down ever since I was told I was a psychic and a mind reader.

"Hon, are you feeling okay?" my mother asked me, sitting down on the sofa and putting her arm around me. That only made me feel worse. Tears started trickling down my cheeks, and, before I knew it, I was having a full-on crying jag.

"Mum, I've been so horrible." I sobbed into her chest, breathing in her soft, flowery scent. My mum made wordless soothing sounds and drew me close. I suddenly wanted to tell her everything so badly, but I knew that she would think I was crazy and call the closest asylum.

"It's okay, Beryl. Nothing you do can be so bad that you can't fix what's been done," my mum said, sounding so different and motherly that I started to cry harder if that was possible.

Once my tears had dried up, I could feel my mother shaking. I leaned back to see tears streaming down her face like an everlasting waterfall. I was quite scared. I had never seen my mother cry that badly before.

She was like an army general to me: strong, powerful, and, most important of all, tearless—oh, and evil and cold-hearted. I reached a finger up and wiped a tear that was trapped in her eyelid like a sparkling jewel.

"Mum? Do you miss Dad?" I asked, looking up into her eyes. I answered my own question easily enough, but I wanted to hear her say it herself. It didn't really mean anything for me to zap it from her mind; I wanted to hear it coming from her mouth. My mother looked like she was arguing with herself inside. She opened her mouth once, closed it again, and then opened it again.

"Yes, Beryl, dear, I do." My mother closed her eyes again, and I felt satisfaction coursing through my veins. Finally, at long last, my mother admitted to me and to herself that she missed him. She hadn't said that she loved him; that would take a lot of work to get out.

In normal family life, the mother and daughter would both hug and comfort each other. Unfortunately for me, I wasn't one of the lucky people on this earth who lead a "normal" life.

The fire alarm started blaring like it would never stop, and smoke started drifting alarmingly into the living room, presumably from the kitchen. God help us all if it's just the dog (aka Adrian) farting again. A second later, my little sister Carla came running into the room babbling incoherently about something not being her fault. I sighed, and lay back, watching my mother run from the room as if a pack of hellhounds were chasing her. A split second later, the door bell rang, shrill and piercing, adding to all the noise in the house.

"Beryl, go see who it is!" my mother screeched from the kitchen. After everything I have gone through today, I have to go and answer the door? My heart pains at the thought of it. I got up grumbling, not yet knowing what terror awaited me, and walked to the front door, bumping dizzily into the glass door.

I opened the door, almost blinded by the light from outside. It was like I was a vampire seeing light for the first time. Sooner or later, I was going to burn up and die. The first thing I saw or heard was not singing angels but—

"Beryl! Get ready to die!" Adira yelled.

Chapter 5

"I can't believe you're doing this to me," I grumbled, my words muffled because of the scarf that was wrapped tightly across my face.

"Relax; you'll enjoy it when you get there! Besides, it's good to know more about your family history!" Adira said cheerfully, still smiling, even though it looked as if someone had stuck sticky tape on the sides of her mouth. Honestly, it wasn't a look I'd go for.

I still couldn't believe that Adira was dragging me half way across London for something that she wouldn't even tell me about. All she'd said was that it'd be good for my fragile state of health. Pfft, I was certainly feeling fragile, but it wasn't exactly about my health, maybe mentally fragile but not physically—whatever. It's not like I was about to hurl myself of the Big Ben anytime soon. "Remind me again why we're not taking the train and making life easier." If I catch pneumonia, she's going to be the one paying all my health bills.

"It's for your health. Fresh air is good for the body." Adira stretched out her arms and took a deep breath in as if to prove her point. I had half a mind to run to the nearest train station and catch the first train that showed up as long as it took me far, far away from wherever Adira was planning to go. I snorted at that but didn't bother to waste my precious breath on her.

After what felt like weeks rather than hours, we finally got to some broken down, old shack way out in the countryside that I wouldn't give a second look at if I was passing by. There was a big sign that read "PRIVATE PROPERTY. KEEP AWAY," written in bold, capital letters. I got the message pretty quickly that we weren't welcome, but I can't say the same for Adira.

She actually looked as if she was considering going inside. I sometimes seriously wonder if Adira has a death wish that she never told me about. If she did, she was on the right road to death. Even as I watched, a window pane collapsed in on itself and the window shattered.

"You think this place looks fun because, to me, all I can see is a dump that will almost certainly kill us if we try and get in there." I turned to Adira accusingly and gave her "The Look."

"It's not half as bad as it looks," Adira said half-heartedly. I got the feeling that Adira had never been there before. To make things easier for me, I looked into Adira's eyes. She *had* never been to this cottage or whatever it was. She was told to go there by some person.

Before I could look deeper into her mind, I felt a sharp pain at the back of my head. The next thing I knew, my head was killing me, and I was sprawled on the floor like an earthquake had hit us. Make that only me. Adira was standing with her arms crossed so tightly across her chest that it seemed unlikely they would unravel in the next couple of years.

"I thought you knew by now that I value my privacy and that I don't appreciate it when it is taken away from me," Adira said, cold fury in every word she spoke. She turned away from me and began to walk in the direction of the hut, her back straight and rigid. She made it clear with every step she took that she didn't give a damn whether I followed her or not.

Adira reached the door and examined it as though she was thinking whether it was safe or not to go inside. I felt guilty. I wouldn't exactly enjoy it if someone barged their way into my mind without my permission and started reading all my personal info. Plus if I didn't follow her, I would be stuck in the middle of marshland. That was when I made my decision.

"Adira! Hey, Adira!" I shouted, my voice echoing. She turned around (possibly out of shock) and gave me a look that was clearly visible even from where I was standing.

"I'm sorry, okay? I won't read your mind again; and I'm sorry I ever did," I meekly said, walking closer to her so I wouldn't have to repeat the word sorry again. To my surprise, Adira didn't cold shoulder me like I thought she would. On the contrary, her face split into a wide smile that was so unlike her that I nearly fell down flat on my face.

She bounded up to me and threw her arms around me like some long lost relative. In reality, she was my long lost relative. When she finally released me from her strangle hold, she beamed at me again.

"Okay. What is going on? Have you been sniffing glue, because it's not good for you." I asked her as soon as I got my breath back. Trust me, if Adira ever hugs you, you would almost definitely be panting like a dog, an old, dying dog at that.

"This shows that you're willing to back down on an argument and that you're willing to go in the right direction with constructive criticism. It shows that you make the right choices, and you can admit that you have done something wrong," Adira reeled off as if she was reading from a very long list.

"*Okay*," I said, trying to make out that I understood what the hell she was talking about. Damn it; the only person who I hadn't had an argument with was going loo-loo, and I can tell you now that it wasn't what you would call a good experience that I could learn from.

"What are we doing here? You haven't exactly told me yet."

"Well, this is the way that people who are not Wrayalis get to Pelesmia, which is where they live," Adira said simply, as if we were discussing last night's episode of *Friends*, which I'm totally obsessed about by the way. She was still looking around like she was Alice in Wonderland, so it was pretty safe to assume that she had been here the same amount of times as me, which is never.

"I'm guessing you've never been here before."

Adira looked at me with the more familiar face of annoyance. At least I had some sort of clue that Adira hadn't turned over to the dark side.

"Duh, there is more than one way to get to Pelesmia." Adira was back to the snobby brat in less than a second. "Jesus Christ, I wish they'd chosen a cleaner way to get there." She gingerly picked up a wooden raft that looked as if it had been eaten by moths and god knows how many more bugs. Just thinking about them makes me feel as if an infestation of fleas were living on me, even though I've never even seen lice in real life (Thank god).

She opened the door carefully, as if scared that the door would fall apart at the slightest touch, and walked inside. I stepped in after her, and what I saw made my mouth drop open and display itself to the world, and I'm guessing that it wasn't a very pretty sight.

The place looked (and smelled) as if it hadn't been cleaned anytime recently. Pieces of what looked like mouldy cheese were strewn across what looked like a living room underneath all of the dust, and the stench was awful. It smelled as if someone had recently died here, and no one remembered to bury the body. Seriously, it was that bad. Adira looked as if she was about to puke; she was all bent up and everything.

"Are you serious? This is the way to get to Pel-whatnot?" I looked over and saw that Adira was gagging too hard to answer me. I could barely hear myself think. When she finally stood up straight, she had a strained look of disgust that made her look like a constipated baboon. I felt tingling in my body and I started to laugh in a strange, high-pitched voice that sounded nothing like me.

Adira looked at me with a look of pure disapproval that reminded me so strongly of my mother that I snorted through my nose; and the sound made me laugh harder. It was almost as if I couldn't stop giggling like a little girl in pigtails on her first day of school. I began to feel strangely light headed, and I fell to the floor, still laughing madly. I noticed that Adira's mouth was hanging open slightly as she stared at me in shock, and, for some reason, this made me laugh harder.

"What are we doing here?" I giggled, completely losing my head. "Do you live here?" Adira's mouth had gone slack as she evidently tried to figure out what was wrong with me. I was in no state to say another word, and I dropped to my knees, gasping for breath. I was acting even worse than a person who'd gone without sleep for a week. In other words, I wasn't acting how sane people are supposed to act.

I couldn't draw enough breath into my lungs. I began to feel decidedly dizzy, and I couldn't breathe properly without feeling a sharp pain in my chest. All I could think about was how stupid it would be to die laughing.

Without a word, Adira marched over to me and grabbed my arm, pulling me up straight. Then she slapped me so hard across the face that I heard what was left of the air in my lungs whooshing out. My face stung badly, and I could feel it turning red and hot under the hand that I had pressed to my face. Trust me, you wouldn't want to get on the wrong side of Adira, or she would slap you back to reality—literally, just like what she did to me unfortunately.

"*Ow!* What was that for?" I yelped, massaging what felt like a broken cheek bone under my left hand. The other hand was pulling on Adira's arm—painfully, I hope. She looked at me steadily, straight in the eye, and I hastily strengthened my mental barriers, not wanting to be left mentally unstable.

"Hey! I'm not laughing like an idiot anymore!" I cried. Adira gave me a look that said that even if I wasn't laughing anymore, I was still acting like I was. I took a deep breath in, finally understanding why my mother had always said not to take things for granted. Like now, I felt like going on my knees and worshiping god for making air.

"Wait . . . why *was* I laughing like an idiot in the first place?" It was true. I could tell that whatever had happened to me before (i.e., laughing like a lunatic) was completely gone.

"This room is infiltrated with Helio gas. It has healing properties and is used in Pelesmia. As you can tell, it makes you unaware of what is going on, and you forget everything that has happened so far in your life." Adira gave me an annoyed look like it was my fault the room had somehow been infiltrated with this Helio gas. Pfft, I'm guessing Adira had never been caught doing anything wrong in her oh-so-perfect life, and if she had been doing anything wrong, she would be out of there like a vampire being chased with holy water.

"That still doesn't explain why I was laughing really hard, and I couldn't stop." I looked at her quizzically, finally registering the look of guilt on her face. "And why the Helio gas had no affect on you at all . . ." At that, Adira looked ready to fall to the ground and beg my forgiveness for whatever reason she was thinking of.

I'm not saying that would be a bad thing or anything, but it would be decidedly awkward. At least I would have a good reason to ask her to be my willing slave for eternity.

"I am truly sorry. I just didn't think." Before I could ask her what she was talking about, she barrelled on as if she wanted to get it all out before she could stop herself. "You see, this shack is full of Helio to repel people from coming in. Mostly, that is what they do; but, for the magically gifted such as yourself, it works slightly differently and can be fatal from lack of oxygen."

I gawped at her, surprised by what she had said. Wow. She really was trying to kill me, only in a very different way to how I thought she would. Believe me; I know which of the deaths I would choose if I had a choice.

"Oh, well, its fine. It's not like you knew there was going to be Helio in here." Adira's look of guilt deepened, and I stared at her incredulously. "Wait . . . you did know there was Helio in here?" To my surprise, Adira began to babble like I had a gun pointed to her head.

"Well, I had a slight thought that there might be, but I didn't think it would affect you the way that it did because I thought that it would behave normally for you, just like it does for me; but I was obviously wrong, so I brought you here; so—" I held up one hand to stop her from talking. It felt like I was some emperor, and

I was silencing my slave (Adira). Jeez, I thought she wouldn't stop talking.

For once, I had a little control over her and I was going to make good use of it. She obviously thought I was going to blab to the Lord or something, so she tried to act like a normal human and apologise—like she would do that if she wasn't afraid I would snitch on her.

"It's all right. *Normal* people"—I put slight pressure on normal— "make mistakes every day. It's natural, and you learn from them, so you don't make the same mistakes again and again." I put on a saintly expression and put my hands together as if I was praying. I felt like a humanities teacher combined with a nun.

Adira gave me a look that said clearly, without me having to read her mind, that she was above normal and that she didn't make mistakes. Wow, ever thought of taking a job as a big head, Adira? I didn't dare to say these words aloud—I did want to make it home all in one piece or, at the very least, alive. I mean, it wasn't much to ask from a person; but, for Adira, I have no idea what she plans on doing to me.

Adira spoke then, breaking my train of thought. "I don't know about you, but I'd rather get out of here before this whole place collapses in on itself." She was right. She didn't add on the fact that the longer we stayed there, the longer we stank of rotten cheese.

"Wait . . . you said earlier on that, somewhere in this shack, there's a way to get to Pelesmia." Adira nodded. "Well, how do we get there?" Adira looked up at the heavens as if asking for help from god. If anyone needed help, it would be me. And I'm talking about mental help.

I carried on relentlessly, not caring if Adira wasn't listening to me. It's easier to make sense of my thoughts when I speak them aloud. That's probably the reason a lot of people at school think I'm more than slightly bonkers.

"If they sent us here, there must be an entrance to Pelesmia from here. All we need to do is find it. I'll go look upstairs, and you look downstairs. If I see anything, I'll call you, and you call me if you find it." I started walking towards the stairs, and then I paused in my tracks as a long lost question popped up in my head.

"Wait! Why do the Wrayalis things even care if the Scroll of Elysium gets stolen?" I asked, scrutinising her perfect face. To my surprise, Adira answered straight away.

"Well, the great Lord Jodreus's wife is a human, and she is very fond of earth, seeing as she grew up here. Plus most of the Wrayalis' are married to women who used to be human a long time ago. They begged and lamented to try and save this planet. Nearly all of them continue to have descendants living on earth," Adira explained steadily. "What goes on in Earth does have an effect on Pelesmia as well, so they would have less love, and anything could happen. Pelesmia functions on love."

"Oh." I turned around and carried on walking towards the narrow staircase, being careful not to touch anything that didn't particularly need to be touched. I could tell that Adira hadn't been listening to a word I'd been saying; but, this time, it'd be her fault if she loses me.

I reached the bottom of the stairs, and I looked up in wonder. I didn't think it was possible for any person's house to be messier than mine, but I was obviously wrong. I think.

I picked my foot up and carefully pressed it down on the first step. I mean, I didn't want the whole staircase to collapse on me; I can't imagine that would be too comfortable. The stairs seemed quite sturdy, so I carried on walking, the stairs creaking as if I was a freaking giant. I am proud to say, without lying, that I didn't fall over even once.

Once I reached the top of the stairs, I looked around in wonder. The upper floor was even filthier than the ground floor, if that was even possible. Dirty pieces of clothing were strewn across the landing as if whoever lived here hadn't had the time of their day to a little bit of cleaning. Either that or they couldn't afford cupboards. There was a long corridor that had different coloured doors lined up, side by side, like soldiers in an army.

I opened the door that was nearest to me, holding my breath, not wanting to throw up and embarrass myself in front of Adira. I'd done that enough times today to last a normal person a lifetime—embarrass myself, I mean. Sadly, the door opened to reveal the worst kept bathroom that I had ever seen in my life, and that was saying something. It was enough to give any sane person nightmares.

I'm not even going to try and explain to you how horrible the toilet looked. Let's just put it this way. A public toilet that you would find on the side of a road was like a five-star haven compared to the muck that lay in front of me.

The bath was tarnished so badly that you could see more black dirt than the white of the bath. The sink was just as bad as the bath, and what looked like green mould was growing on the sides. It was seriously gross.

I hastily slammed the door shut and took a deep breath in. The mouldy air of the corridor smelled like sweet perfume compared to the stench of the bathroom. I looked at the next door that was patterned with fading, twining roses. It looked innocent enough, but I had to literally force my hand up to grasp the brass doorknob. I dreaded seeing whatever lay in there. After what I had already seen today, it couldn't have been anything good.

Bracing myself, I twisted the handle and was about to push the door open when a glimmer of gold caught my gaze. It was an intricately designed piece of art that was so detailed and good that I would expect to find it in an art gallery and not in some rambling shack in the middle of nowhere.

What looked like a face so full of beauty and life that it nearly made me cry was etched on the rotting wood of the door, which somehow made the piece of work seem more beautiful than I knew it was. It had a type of magic to it that made me know that no normal artist could ever make something as beautiful as this.

Flowers were tattooed on the side of her face, but it enhanced her austere features. I stared transfixed at it, not knowing how long I stood there with my mouth hanging slightly open like a dunce. It could have been seconds, minutes, or even hours. I couldn't seem to make myself turn away. It was like I was in a trance.

At least five minutes had passed when I finally registered in my mind that something was jabbing me in the ankle—hard. I tried to ignore it, afraid that if I looked away, the image would disappear. I glanced down quickly, tearing my gaze away from the door. A broken piece of metal lying on its side was poking me painfully.

I kicked it aside, and, once more, I focused on the carving. At least I tried to, seeing as it wasn't there anymore. I raked the door frantically with my eyes, searching for the art desperately. I badly wanted to see it again, feeling a sense of loss when I couldn't find it. It was quite silly really, seeing as I'd never liked art at school.

This carving was different though. It made me feel calm and peaceful inside, which was a nice change from the usual turmoil that I usually felt. I felt like crying when it became obvious that I wouldn't be able to find it. I shook my head like dog that had come out of water, trying to get control over my thoughts.

It just wasn't possible for a piece of art to just vanish from a door. Wait. Let me correct myself. It's not possible for a carving to vanish in a world where psychics, flying men, and all the other ladida in the world didn't exist. It was probably normal in Adira's world.

I opened the door, no longer afraid of what would be inside there. I was secretly hoping that there would be more carvings like the one on the door. If there were, I would have gone straight home, packed some clothes and food, and moved to live in this room. That's how amazing the art was.

Of course, seeing how my luck went, the walls were bare, except for the same twining roses that were on the door outside. Thank god the room didn't smell half as bad as the landing. There was a bed in the middle of the spacious room, and the covers and carpet were coated with a thin lining of dust. Other than that, the room didn't have anything else inside except for the chest of drawers.

I was about to leave the room when a flash of gold caught my eye. I turned around, desperate to see another carving or painting and to feel that strange calmness again. What I saw was just as beautiful and breathtaking but not exactly what I expected to see.

A beautifully sculpted urn was standing on top of the chest of drawers, resting so it couldn't have fallen. The lid was not in place on the top of the urn, but it was lying on its side next to it. I took a step closer to it to examine it. It appeared to be made of solid gold, and black patterns were engraved delicately onto it. I was prepared at that point to bet on my life that, when I first went inside the room, it wasn't there.

"Adira! Come up here for a sec!" I yelled. "I'm in the second door to the left!" I walked a couple more steps nearer to the urn, holding my breath, this time, from excitement. I stopped one foot away from the urn, afraid of what would happen if I touched it.

Adira still hadn't come, so I figured that I might as well look and see what was inside it.

I took a deep breath, took one more step closer, and bent my head to look inside. It was empty. Disappointment flooded inside of me, almost drowning me.

I was about to raise my head, but I found that I couldn't. Panic welled inside of me, and I frantically tried to move my frozen limbs. I could feel myself slowly sinking into the urn, and I was almost blinded with panic. I yelled Adira's name one last time before I was hurtling through what seemed to be a long, never ending tunnel.

Suffocating darkness pressed in from all sides, and I would have screamed if I could. Problem was that I couldn't make a sound. I could see a blinding white light at the end of it; and I leaned forward, eager to be able to see again, completely forgetting everything that my mother had told me about not stepping into the light (death). If this was how blind people have to live each day, I am so grateful to god that I've got perfect vision. Well, nearly perfect.

With a thump that should have broken every bone in my body, I hit soft, mossy ground. I lay there on the floor, panting heavily. I felt myself carefully, checking that all my bones were intact.

"Jeez, ever try to land delicately?" Birdie's voice piped from inside of me. Now she talks to me? After everything that had happened, she kept silent; and, now, she tries to speak to me?

I figured that as Birdie was a part of me, she would be able to hear my thoughts. Just to make sure that she knew what I thought of her, I repeated everything that I was thinking aloud. Shockingly, Birdie had the nerve to stay quiet and act as if she had suddenly gone deaf again. That's it. As soon as this whole mess is over, I will dedicate my life to finding out how to get rid of Inlai.

I stood up carefully and stretched my body out. I seemed to be standing on the top of a grassy hill. Great, trust me to end up on the top of a hill, not having a clue where I was. I inwardly slapped myself. Why on earth did I look inside? It wasn't exactly normal to find a priceless urn in a shack. Now, I was on the top of a hill in some place that I had never been to before. I sighed and did the inevitable. I walked down. Seeing how mountain hiking wasn't exactly on my list of hobbies, it took me a lot longer than the average person to walk down. The sound of a busy village was getting louder and louder until I could feel the noise reverberating through my body.

The sounds of laughter and chattering people hit me like a wave. I leaped off from the bottom of the hill and walked towards what appeared to be a village. I strode inside and tried to look as if I knew where I was and what the hell I was doing here.

It struck me how different this village was, compared to the villages that I had been to. For one thing, the people living in this place actually looked happy to be there. Children were skipping around in circles, playing some sort of game that involved ropes and what looked like a ball . . .

Stalls lined the sides of the streets, selling all sorts of goods. Old fashioned cottages with thatched roofs and all lined the sides of the street. There were people everywhere I looked—women bustling around, holding children's hands, kids playing all sorts of games, and what appeared to be barnyard animals strutting their stuff.

It occurred to me how differently they were dressed compared to what I was wearing. The women were wearing long dresses, which had sleeves that were extra long. They were faded colours and had a feeling of being secondhand. Some of the younger children had bonnets on as well.

The men wore shirts with a leather vest over. They had cropped trousers on with stockings underneath. It was like being back in the Tudor times, only without all the blood and guts. If you ask me, that's just as well.

The village itself looked as if it had been cut out from a children's story book; that's how odd everything seemed to me—nice but odd. I looked down at myself, realising how strange I must seem to the people. Never mind how weird they looked, I probably looked as if I had come down to earth on a spaceship.

Even though I was only wearing jeans and a t-shirt, I could feel disapproval radiating from the people like I was wearing a short skirt and a leather jacket. Pfft, I would pay a lot of money to see these people's faces if they ever got to see Genevieve Brockwell, the school snob. Her school skirt, which is supposed to be knee-length, is so short that it could easily be mistaken for a thick belt. I'm not even exaggerating.

Just as I was thinking these less than lovely thoughts, a boy who couldn't be a day older than five walked towards me. He was so small that he had to bend his head back to look at me, and I wasn't what you would call a BFG. I tried to pull up my mental barriers, and when I couldn't, I panicked. It took me a good minute to figure out that they were already up.

"My name's Arthur, and I'm gonna be six in two months and fourteen days," he said, sticking out a chubby hand and grasping mine. "Why are you wearing that?"

I looked down at him, surprised, and it wasn't just because of his age. He had a cute button nose with freckles sprinkled across it. Dark brown hair poked out of his hat, and his navy blue eyes sparkled up at me in a carefree manner that only a child could have.

I let go of his hand, realising that I still had it in my grasp. I looked down at him, unsure of what to say. I mean, I couldn't tell him the truth. If I did, he'd run of to his mama screaming and tell the whole world. He was, after all, only five years old as he'd so kindly told me.

Just as I opened my mouth to speak to him, a very harassed looking woman, whose buttons were done up wrong, grabbed Arthur by the shoulders and shook him hard.

"Arthur! What do you think you are doing! I wake up from my afternoon nap to find the house empty and with no trace as to where you were! You could have been dead for all I knew!" His mum ranted on about how worried she'd been and why he would do that to her. She didn't even seem to notice me standing less than half a metre behind them.

I waited for about two minutes, not wanting to be rude, but when Arthur's mother gave no hint of stopping her lecture anytime soon, I backed away as quietly as I could. Seeing how I had never been one of the luckier people, I was bound to mess up in my evil plan of escaping. Sure enough, I stepped on a branch that snapped noisily under my shoes. I froze.

Arthur's mother stopped midflow, and turned to look at me, more like gawp at me. Arthur smiled gleefully at me, his eyes lighting up with mischief. He was evidently glad to be out of trouble so soon. Huh. I'm glad someone's happy to have me here. Unfortunately, Arthur's mum wasn't as glad to see me.

"And who are you, young lady?" she asked me, her eyes, which were a stormy gray colour, glared down at me. To be honest, as scared as I was, I couldn't really blame her for being annoyed with me. Think about it. Imagine you were a mother who'd lost your five-year-old son, and then you find him chatting with a teenage girl who you'd never seen before in your life. If I ever found my son doing that, he wouldn't live to tell the story.

I arranged my face into what I hoped was a sweet smile and stuck out my hand in greeting. I checked that my mental barriers were extra strong and looked her in the eye, knowing that people were more likely to trust you if you looked them in the eye rather than at the ground.

Arthur's mum looked surprised at my display of politeness. She shook my hand cautiously, as if it would suddenly turn into a venomous snake and bite her.

"Um, I'm Beryl, Beryl Jones." When she carried on staring at me blankly, I let down my mental barriers for a split second, catching a glimpse of her mind. She was surprised because she thought she knew all of the people in this village. I hurried on in my explanation.

"You wouldn't know me. I'm not from around here." If only she knew. A look of comprehension dawned on her face. I smiled, glad that she had finally understood what I was talking about.

"You must be from the Jones family from Sweden! I thought that you were coming here in the next week! I'm Lizette, but everybody round here calls me Lizzie." Guess I spoke to soon. Lizzie shook my hand vigorously and smiled at me more warmly than I had seen her act before. I opened my mouth to correct her, but something told me not to. I closed it again. Lizzie seemed to be oblivious to anything but her son, whose shirt she was tucking in.

"So, where's the rest of your family?" She asked me, turning her head to face me. I frantically racked my brains, trying to think up a lie that would sound slightly normal.

"They're, uh, coming next week."

"Really? What made you come early?" she looked Arthur over, deemed him acceptable, and gave him a little shove towards the playground. Her curly brown hair had slipped from the tie on the top of her head, and she was now hastily tying it back up. It was almost like her hands were always doing something, and if they had nothing to do, they would be playing a game with themselves. It was like she had ADHD. Thankfully, I had an answer ready.

"I came early to see the scenery that you are so well known for." I tried to mimic the throaty tone of voice that most of the people round here had. Lizzie laughed, not unkindly. It was a sweet sound that made her seem years younger than she really was.

"I could show you the most beautiful place in the whole world if you want. It's where my parents first met," she said dreamily, curling a strand of hair around her index finger. I stared at her, realising that she couldn't be more than a couple of years older than me, and yet she had a five-year-old son.

I do not want to think how that could have happened. It seemed to me that round here, in this place, people have children early and make friends easily and quickly. Man, I love this place already. Lizzie took my silence as hesitation, and quickly backed down on her offer.

"You don't have to come if you don't want to. I just thought—"

"No, I'd love to come." She smiled and linked arms with me.

"So where do you want to—" Lizzie began but was cut off by a scream. I turned around, swivelling Lizzie around with me. Seeing how wide her eyes were, I gathered that I wasn't the only one who had heard the scream. I strained, listening for anything.

Lizzie grabbed Arthur, who had been skipping in circles around us, and held him close. The scream came again, this time, distinctly louder. I was about to lower my mental barriers to try and see who it was, but something inside me told me not to lower them. Instead, I made them stronger.

It seemed as if the whole village had gone silent and frozen. The playground was empty as all of the children had gone running to their mummies. I couldn't blame them, to be honest. If I knew where my mother was, I would have gone running to her long before now.

I was about to take a step closer to the hill to see who it was, but before I could move, a woman came running into sight. Her wildly curling bright red hair stood up from her head as if she had been electrified. Her deep, sea blue eyes, wide with terror, darted across the village, searching for danger. When she could see that there wasn't any, she ran towards me and Lizzie, which wasn't really surprising seeing as we were the only people left on the outskirts of the village.

The woman grabbed the front of my shirt and held on hard as if she was holding on to her life string. Lizzie made it as if to yank me free, but something in the woman's expression must have told her that she meant no harm or something like that as she took a step towards me but made no sign to free me.

I began to feel slightly scared now. A crazy woman with rose tattoos on the side of her face was practically carrying me by the front of my shirt and was doing nothing except gaze into my eyes like a newborn child gazing at her mother for the first time.

Even though I was absolutely sure that I had never seen this woman before, she looked oddly familiar. I looked around and saw that everyone had frozen—literally. Their eyes were wide and staring, and their bodies were rigid. Only the woman was moving.

She released me and held my hands, which were now sweating like crazy, in a vice grip.

"I know who you are." Her voice came out in a high, girlish twitter. It took me a split second to figure out what she said.

"How do you—"

"Never mind that. Go back to where you belong. It is not safe for you to stay here." The woman began muttering under her breath, presumably some voodoo magic to send me back to reality. "Wait. Who are you?" I blurted out, desperate to know who this woman was and what she was doing here.

"You know." As she said the last word, I felt a whooshing sensation, and it wasn't because of what she had just said. This woman was Aya. Before I could say another word, I felt a jerk from behind me, and I could hear a whistling sound as I was thrown back to my time. I hit the floor of the bedroom with a loud thud that should have made the windows shatter and started an earthquake in Australia. I lay there on the floor, shock pumping through my body, right next to my heart.

Don't ask me how I knew it, but one thing's for sure; the woman, who had been right next to me a second ago, was the legendary Aya.

CHAPTER 6

"Beryl? Are you all right ?" Adira's voice drifted through my mind. I could tell from the sound of her muffled voice that she was still downstairs. How considerate. She hears an earth shaking thud and doesn't even bother to come up and check if I was still alive. What *are* friends for? I never got to hear the answer to that question. That's probably because there isn't one.

My head was full to bursting point with what I was sure was world changing information. Well, at least for me. I didn't bother to try and answer her; I simply lay on the floor with my face mashed up in the carpet.

I took in a deep breath which was pretty hard to do seeing as I was sprawled face down on the floor. That wasn't exactly a good idea as the carpet smelled like it hadn't been cleaned recently, if ever. I choked and sat up straight, gasping for breath. Trust me on this;

you do *not* want to smell dirty old carpets in your free time. They stink like 'ell.

"Beryl?" Adira's voice had gotten louder than it had been before. The door banged open and Adira walked inside, her face elated like she had just won Euro millions. I wish. I could've stolen all the money of off her.

"You will never believe what I—what do you think you're doing on the floor? Now's not exactly a good time to have an afternoon nap." Adira stood in the door way, not bothering to come help me up.

"Oh, ha, ha, very funny . . . Do you think you could lend me a hand? My butt is killing me." I may not be an old granny, but I sure as hell wasn't made out of stone. Adira, of course, was not prone to that little fact, judging from her snort that, I'm guessing, said "not in a million years." And guess what? I was right, shocking.

"Help yourself up. You got yourself onto the floor; you get yourself off the floor." Jeez, some people these days just don't understand the rules of life. Number one: *help one another*. Someone should seriously explain that to Adira. I doubt it would help her in any way though, seeing as she was the most stubborn person I had ever met in my entire life and that was saying something. All you had to do was look at the people that I've grown up with. I heaved myself of the floor, mumbling to myself about young people these days, even though, technically, she was over seven hundred years old.

"Wait . . . what were you doing on the floor?" Adira's face was a complete question mark, as if she had just realised the position I was in when she found me on the floor. "You looked as if you were praying or something." Ha, if I'd been praying, it would've been for fresh air and the chance to live again.

I considered for a second not telling her what had just happened; she kept more than enough secrets from me herself. For once, I would know something before she did. I mean, she was bound to torture it out of me one way or another. The shock and confusion of what had just happened was still too much for me to make head or tail of the recent events, and I did want to get what was going on around here. So I opened my big mouth and told her everything.

"Whoa. Whoa." That seemed all that Adira was capable of saying. I waited impatiently to hear her speak proper English. When it seemed all she could do was mouth wordlessly like a goldfish, I butted in.

"So what do you think this means?" I asked Adira eagerly. Adira closed her mouth, which had been gaping at me, not unlike the way Adrian looks whenever I ask him a simple question. She looked as if she was thinking hard, and she massaged her temples while she thought. A whole minute had passed, and I wasn't what you would call patient.

"Well?"

"Are you 100% sure that the woman you saw just now was Aya?" Adira's voice made it sound like she doubted my sanity. "I mean, Aya died like a gazillion years ago, so—"

"I am absolutely sure." I felt for just a second, deep in my gut, that I was right. "Definitely."

"Did you know that the shack that we are both standing in right now used to be the place where Aya and her family lived?" Adira looked up at me finally. I didn't get what the history of where Aya used to live was of any importance, but I didn't think Adira would take that *too* lightly.

"No, I didn't. But I don't see what that has to do with—"

"It has everything to with it. Now shut up and listen to me." Adira glared at me, and I closed my mouth quickly, wanting to still have a full set of teeth by the time I went home.

"Aya's home village, Ciute, was destroyed, as you should know." I sent up a mental thank-you note to Ms. Sparks.

"Aya still felt a strange connection with the place where she had spent her childhood. She went back to visit Ciute, but all that was left was an old shack that had once been the home of her family. Amazingly, it stood whole and complete as if the war had happened in some other place. She couldn't bear not to have at least one memory of her hometown. She set enchantments on it to make it capable of staying intact until the world ended. By doing so, Aya endangered her own life. Enchantments like those take great amounts of your energy, and if you don't know when to stop, you could end up dead you know," She said matter-of-factly.

I stared at her, thinking she was finished. I was about to speak when Adira gave me an annoyed look that clearly said she wasn't done yet. She continued.

"It didn't stop her from coming regularly to the shack, though, to meditate and draw. No one knows exactly what she did when she came here; she took no one with her and told no person what she did. It is still unclear, even now, what she did. All that is known is that she was found dead here in this shack."

Adira paused to lean against the chest of drawers. I took the silence as an invitation to do what I did best-talk.

"Wait . . . You said that Aya drew and meditated when she came here, right?" Adira nodded cautiously, wondering where all this was leading on to.

"I think I may have seen one of them" Adira's mouth went slack for the second time in a row, and, this time, I didn't really blame her.

"That can't be possible. They're said to come in and out of existence, and it's really hard, almost impossible, to see one." Adira was shaking her head with disbelief. To be honest, that is exactly what I would have said if I was her. If I was her, I probably would have had the same reaction. Imagine being told that some teenage girl had seen a legendary piece of art that may not even exist. Pfft, I would call the nearest asylum.

This was different though. I really *had* seen that carving. It would be impossible to forget how amazing and detailed it would be. I can't just make things up like that. Even I'm not that good of a liar.

"Adira, you have to trust me on this." I looked meaningfully into her eyes, trying to convey some sort of message through to her without speaking. Trouble was that Adira was a stone head; you had to repeat everything that wasn't natural ten million times before it could get through to her; and, even then, she still wouldn't listen. At the end of the day, she is, after all, just a rock.

To my surprise, I read hesitation in her eyes as she struggled with her thoughts. For a split second, I could see that she was unsure, and then I saw resolution. I held my breath as I waited for what she was going to say.

"Okay then. Even though I think you're of your rocker, it does make sense." I stared at Adira incredulously. Heck, this whole thing happened to me, and I still don't get what on earth happened back then. If it was possible to go back in time, then I would sort of get it; but get real. This is the twenty first century for god's sake. You can't go zooming around backwards and forwards in time, maybe in the year three thousand but not now.

At least that's what I used to think before I was told I was a psychic. Anything's probably possible now. Wait. Let me correct myself. *Everything is possible now.* Adira's voice cut in on my daydream, sending me back to reality.

"Tell me exactly what was on the 'carving' you saw." I could hear the quotation marks hanging over the word "carving." I felt myself bristling in annoyance. I seriously hate it when people don't believe me when I say something that is perfectly true. I mean, okay, I have been known to lie more than once in my life, but it gets on my nerves when the one time I make an effort to tell the truth, no one believes me.

"Well, there was this picture of some woman, but it was different to what people normally look like. There was something about that carving that made me want to stay here and stare at that carving for all eternity. If joy could ever be drawn as human, the person that would come straight to mind would be her." Great, now I sounded like a freaking poet. All I need to do now is find out how to bring Shakespeare back to life and marry him. We'd win the poets of the year award.

"She had roses tattooed on to the side of her face, but, for some reason, it made her look more beautiful than she really was. Plus the whole thing was engraved into some really old, rotting wood, but it didn't look any worse than it would have if it was sculpted into new wood." I stared at Adira defiantly. No one can listen to that and still think I'm lying. If they did, they can go and boil themselves in oil. Same thing goes for Adira, but I'd give her the choice of water or oil, though I'm guessing none of them would feel too good.

"Yeah, that's what the stories all say. She whittled wood so beautifully and skilfully that it seemed to have a sort of magic about them. Everything you just said is completely true. The woman you saw was probably Aya. She was well known for her love of carving self portraits and her family in wood. It was her way of saying that this was their property, and anyone else who entered was an intruder unless they had direct permission."

Now that she said it that way, the woman in the wood *did* kind of look like the woman that had grabbed me and nearly had my death on her hands (i.e. having a heart attack).

"Wait, hold up a sec. Why are we talking about legendary carvings when we could be figuring out . . . the thing that happened to me?" I was honestly *befuddled*. I love that word. It even sounds confusing. Anyway, I didn't get it though. What *was* the point of talking about missing art pieces? I mean, I get the point that they're nice and all, but, at the end of the day, they were just pictures carved in old rotten wood. What I was not expecting was Adira's flash of anger at my lack of sense, according to her anyway.

"Haven't you been listening to a word of what I've been saying?" Adira hurled at me like she was trying to hurt me—not likely.

"Hard not to with you yelling every two minutes," I murmured under my breath. Adira ignored me in a way that I was getting used to. She must have heard me, if her eyes narrowing in distaste were any clue.

"You need to understand and know who Aya really is under her image. If you don't understand her, how will you have a chance of trying to figure out the weird things that happen which are nearly always connected with Aya?" Adira stared at me, daring me to go against her; but, to be honest, that was the last thing on my mind.

Even though she sounded like a demented psychiatrist, what she was saying did make sense. You have to know the person before you try and figure out their riddles, especially if you've never met them before. In my case, I had seen her, and she said like five words to me, but I wouldn't really count that as a formal meeting. For one thing, I just thought she was some mad old hag and not one of my ancestors.

"Yeah, but you've already told me Aya's life story practically. What else do I need to know?" I asked indifferently. To my surprise, Adira flushed bright red, and I'm guessing that it wasn't from embarrassment. She actually looked quite proud of herself now that I think about it.

"What?" I didn't understand why she was smiling like she had won the Olympics. Of course, Adira didn't feel the need to help me out in figuring why she looked proud. I mean, we were just talking about Aya, and it wasn't like she would suddenly yell "I'm the real Aya!" to tell the truth; I wouldn't be surprised if she was Aya. Too many weird things have happened to me today, and this would be like a piece of cake comparing it to everything.

Before I could ask her what the hell was happening, Adira held out her hand like some sort of queen, waiting for me to shut my (in her opinion) big mouth.

"Look what I found," Adira said smugly as if she was going to meet the queen in person. "Wait a sec." She walked out of the room as if to get something. Can't she tell me the slightest little thing once in a while? It would seriously help me—a lot.

Adira walked back into the room holding a large book or a journal of some sort. It looked really old and fragile, as if it hadn't been used for the last couple millenniums. In fact, it probably hadn't.

What I didn't get was what this had to do with Aya and why Adira was holding it like it was some sort of trophy. I stared dumbfounded at her while she beamed at me, clearly proud of her self. I just wish I knew the reason why.

"Well?"

"Well what?" Adira was clearly disappointed by my reaction. Well, what did she expect? I had no freaking idea what the thing in her hand was. It could be an old math exercise book for all I knew.

"What is it? Is it some kind of spell book or something?" I knew I was totally off the mark when I saw Adira's expression, but it was the only thing that I could think of. I'm not even joking.

"This is the diary of Aya, genius. She kept a journal throughout her life, hoping that, someday, someone would find it and know her life story. She wanted people to know the true story of her suffering and how the war of the tribes truly affected her people." That's it. Adira has completely lost the plot. She might as well have told me that she was an undercover agent working for the FBI. That'd be easier to believe.

"How can you be so sure?" For god's sake, Aya had died like a gazillion years ago like Adira had so kindly mentioned. Plus paper can't stay intact for that long. They rot away one way or another. Oh. Wait. Aya had probably set one of her freaky enchantments to make it *indestructible*!

"While you were up here, lumbering through history, I read a couple of pages. They're written in a different language though, so I'll probably have to translate most of the things written here." I still wasn't convinced. I swear I'd better start looking into mental institutes before Adira tries to kill me. I've still got a life to live, even though it wasn't turning out to be what I'd expected. Adira must've noticed that I still didn't exactly believe her. She stood up and shoved the journal into my lap.

"Do you want to know why I'm not a raving lunatic?" I seriously want to know why, but I wasn't too sure that Adira would appreciate me saying so. "Look at that in the corner of the cover!" I looked closely at the page, not wanting to give her any motive to kill me.

I saw something that looked like some sort of old-fashioned coat of arms. I looked closer, surprised at the intricate pattern of roses that twined itself around the outside like some sort of border. There were two swords making a cross in the centre of the shield. They looked so sharp that I was almost certain that if I touched one of them, it would cut my finger. I was about to look closer when Adira snatched the book from my grasp.

"You see what that is?" Adira half-snarled half-grumbled.

"It's some sort of coat of arms or something."

"Exactly! Aya put this on each and every one of her possessions in everlasting ink! If this doesn't convince you, then god damn you!" I looked at her for a minute, not reading her mind. Like I said, I want to live and grow old.

I thought about what had happened to me in the last few weeks. Unbelievable things had happened, some so strange that I had thought I was having hallucinations. I had no trouble believing them (maybe a little), and they all turned out to be true. Plus, when I'd been the one who was saying unbelievable things that had no proof whatsoever other than my word, she believed me. Oddly (and unfairly), I wouldn't believe her when her idea had logic behind it, whereas my theory shouldn't even be possible.

I shook my head, checking my brain was still intact. I should really stop doing that. I've lost enough brain cells to last a lifetime. I could tell that Adira was aching to find out what was written in the diary, but I was a bit of a problem. Adira looked as if she was ready to walk out the room and figure everything out all by herself, but all I can say to that is *"no way."*

There was no chance that I was going to let Adira get all the fun while I was at home with no one for company other than my alienated mother and messed-up siblings. Nuh-uh, like that was ever going to happen. I think I'd kill myself.

"Okeydokey, if you say that this old thing really is the diary of a woman I never knew existed before the past few weeks, then it is." I waited for Adira's face to break out in a beaming smile that would put the sun to shame. Unfortunately, I was going to have to wait a couple of years for that to ever happen.

All I got was some sort of grimace. Adira turned her full attention back to the journal that despite being older than the largest number I know looked quite good for its age. It might have had Botox though. You never know. My grandma used to always say "nothing that old can look that good." All I can say now is that she was utterly and completely wrong. All you have to do is steal a fairy wand and turn yourself into a princess.

Adira slowly turned a page so carefully and gently that I was forcibly reminded of my Aunt TG while handling her six month baby. I seriously hope she didn't get real hands-on experience while dealing with babies.

I leaned closer to see what was written inside, but I couldn't make out a single letter. Adira was right. The writing was written in some weird curling handwriting that I was certain I had never seen before in my life, which was impressive since I'm kind of a foreign languages freak. It looked oddly like hieroglyphics, only it was slightly more elegant and . . . joined up.

I was bursting to read and find out for myself what was written there, but, sadly, my foreign languages expertise didn't stretch to include languages spoken before dinosaurs and god knows what else.

"What is written down there?" I asked, my curiosity getting the better of me. I mean, it wasn't everyday that you got the chance to read the thoughts and feelings of a long lost ancestor. Plus I didn't even know there were people before the dinosaurs, let only my great (times a million) grandmother who was one of them.

I was not going to let this opportunity slip through my fingers. "Can you just read the passages out loud?" When Adira didn't say anything, I tacked on the word "please" thoughtfully.

You can't get any politer than that. If Adira still wouldn't tell me what was scrawled on the parchment, I was going to have to read her mind and endure whatever she was going to do to me while I was in her head. To tell the truth, I didn't even care whether she was going to turn into Jackie Chan and karate my face off. I just wanted to see what was in the journal.

It didn't make sense to me why I was so desperate to read this thing. It only came to me after that I had wanted to feel some sort of connection with Aya and to know that I was not alone. That sounds like corny and cheesy mixed in with butter, but it *was* the truth.

"Please always helps." I stared at her for a second completely forgetting what we were talking about. I stuck my tongue out at her, more than a little late. Oh well, better late than never. Adira took in a deep breath as if she was going to read a long story. I sat on the bed comfortably, trying not to think about the fact that the bed I was sitting on hadn't been cleaned since Aya was alive, and that had been quite a long time ago.

"This could take a while to translate, so all I ask is that you remain patient." Pfft, she sounded like an air hostess and not in a good way. She scanned the page quickly, translating it as best as she could. She couldn't have taken more than a couple of minutes, but it felt like hours.

She looked up for a split second that clearly told me that she was ready. I could hardly contain myself with excitement. Adira began what I hoped would be a very, very, very long story.

Dear Kitty,

The best thing ever happened to me, even better than jumping in the sea. This is what happened: I was walking down the street as usual on Sunday morning, going to mass, when I found the oddest thing. It looked like some sort of paper thing, but I couldn't really tell; Mummy was holding onto my hand like I was going to jump of the nearest cliff. I wish Alfred would. Then he wouldn't keep using my stuff.

I still don't get why Mummy won't let me use my powers. She said it was dangerous and could hurt someone, but I would never try to hurt someone, maybe Eliza and Beth but no one else.

Anyway, I pretended I needed to pee, but I just went to the paper. I don't know why, but it felt really special. So I picked it up and rolled all of the creases out, but there was nothing written there. I was about to put it in the bin, but then some words came onto it like someone behind me was writing.

It was way creepy. It said something like "Show us your heart's desire." The words faded, and then it showed me getting some sort of reward from Mrs. O'Neill, and my mother and father were both standing next to me, even though Daddy's dead; and Mum was hugging me, saying I was the best daughter she ever had.

It was really nice, and I would have carried on looking, but Mum realised that I was no-where near the loo. I threw it somewhere in the bushes, and I can't find it now. It's really nice though. I think it shows us what we most want.

I miss Daddy, and I hope he knows I still love him and that I didn't want him to die. Mum's yelling at me now to put the candles out and sleep. Honestly, Mummy's gotten so strict now. I hope she still loves me. I'm gonna sleep now before Mummy kills me. Night night.

I stared at Adira, shocked to my core. Had that really been my ancestor talking/writing in a nine-year-old girl version? I didn't understand why I suddenly felt like crying, even though all I'd done was listen to a little girl's diary being read aloud.

I blinked furiously, like I had a bee stuck in my lashes, while Adira flicked through the pages, less cautious than she had been before now that she was certain they weren't suddenly going to rip in half.

"That diary entry was made when she was 8 years old—she wrote her age at the top of each page," Adira said casually. "She wrote in her journal every day of her life until she passed away. This one was made on her death bed." Adira flicked to the very end of the book and scanned the page again.

I felt like yanking my hair out. It was really frustrating not being able to read the diary and understand it for myself. I couldn't even be sure that Adira was translating them correctly, and she wasn't exactly doing her best to translate it as fast she could. Now I know how babies feel, seeing as Adira was treating me like one.

"Okay. She was 98 when she died. This is how it goes." Adira began.

Dear Kitty,

Every part of me aches, my head especially. I feel even worse than I did yesterday. Even though it hurts to admit it to myself, I know I'm going to die soon, and if not today, tomorrow. My bones feel all weak and trembly like they're going to collapse under me at any minute. Jack and Grace are getting really scared. Bless them, they have no one else left in the world except for me ever since their dear parents died.

For the sake of them, I have to walk around the house and act normal and cheerful, even though I feel as if I'm going to collapse at any minute. I hope there is a kind enough soul out there to take good care of them.

The only person I can truly trust is dear old Lizzie, though she's getting on a bit. There's always Arthur and Georgia left, but they can barely remember to feed themselves, let alone young children that need a parental figure in their lives. Oh, I feel all of a sudden faint now.

Lizzie would kill me if she knew how I was worrying. She came over earlier this morning in a hurry because Arthur's hand fast was today, and she didn't want to be late.

I tried to gather up the energy to go, but my arthritis caught me up while going to the carriage. It's just as well. I don't really think anybody would be too anxious to see me after what they found out earlier.

Lizzie sent me straight back to the house, the way my mother used to do whenever I did something naughty. I didn't want to go back home though. I want to die in the place where I was born, my first and true home.

I couldn't leave Jack and Grace by themselves though, so I took them to where I once lived and belonged. Oh, those were the good old days. I don't know how Gracie feels about this; she was never one for moving places ever since her parents died, but I think she's coping.

Jack has always been an odd boy; he was thrilled to come here and see what old Granny got up to.

Dear old Lizzie would kill me if she knew how much energy I had had to use to transport me and the kids here. Oh no, Gracie is crying again. I'd better go and see what's wrong with her. This might be the last time I ever get to write this down. Forever, night-night."

Adira looked up at me with troubled eyes. I let out my breath in a whoosh of air. I felt like crying more than ever. I blinked hard again, and, beside me, Adira roughly wiped her eyes with the back of her wrist. You can't really blame us though. Imagine reading your grandmother's death day.

She sounded like a sweet person whose first priority was family. Great, I sound like Weepy William in *Horrid Henry*. I suddenly felt a rush of loss even though I had never met her before.

"Is there anything else?" My voice broke near the end. God, I was acting worse than I had when I watched Titanic for the first time. I still cry every time I watch it, even though I have seen it ten times by now.

I shook myself. I was being silly now. If my mother was here, she would have beaten me silly with a metal cane. At least, the old version of my mother would. This new Mum would probably hug me and say that everything was going to be okay. I know which one I prefer.

"No, there's nothing. It just says, *'with love,'* at the end." Adira seemed just as annoyed with herself for crying. It was all right for her to cry though. The same thing might have happened to her a couple of centuries ago, minus the diary thing though. She didn't strike me as a *"Dear diary"* person. Don't ask me why; all you have to do is meet her.

I didn't know what to say. I could tell that Adira was just as clueless as I was. I spoke first, unable to bear the awkward silence that was deepening every second. Now I get why people sometimes call silence pregnant. The baby is hell.

"We better go now. Isn't there any chance of you being able to somehow make this diary a little more . . . readable?" I asked, desperate for the chance to be able to read more of Aya's life.

To be honest, I had no hope that even superwoman Adira would be able to do that. To my surprise, she nodded. Is she crazy? The diary had probably affected her more than I thought it had.

"Yeah, there is. I was just being a snob earlier on." Adira had just called herself a snob! This should honestly make the headlines. So she doesn't think she's a perfect little princess. Before I could ask her if she was feeling all right, she took the diary that I hadn't noticed was in my hands and closed it. She pressed a palm on either side of the book, and began speaking in gobbledegook.

"Hunamasifa li teron wai Englo chi chunada lu lai." Adira chanted over and over again while staring at the cover of the book like she wanted to burn a hole right through it. She probably could. I wouldn't be surprised if she started jumping around the book in circles, dancing. The book glowed an eerie blue colour after she said the last "lai," and I nearly jumped out of the window when Adira dropped it into my lap.

"There. It's in a language you will understand." I groaned inwardly. Knowing Adira, she was bound to translate it into Spanish or something like that or, at the very least, French. To my surprise, when the book fell open, I could see that it was in English. I looked up to thank Adira, but there was no one there to thank.

"Adira?" I yelled, my voice echoing. There was no reply. I knew this was too good to be true. She may have translated the diary, but she wasn't going to give me a ride home. Great, I was in what was probably a haunted shack with no idea how to get home. Whoopee! I've got three and a half hours of walking around London, not knowing where the hell I'm going and look forward to. Guess we weren't going to Pelesmia today . . .

*   *   *

"Beryl? Where on earth have you been? I've been worried sick. Do have any idea what time it is? You could have been dead for all I knew!" My mother shrieked. I knew she tried to hide the little tremble she gave at the word dead, and I could tell that she was still sore about Dad dying.

Sheesh, get over it woman! Your ex-husband died two months ago! That is exactly what I wanted to yell at her, but I didn't think she would take that too lightly. Plus I wasn't exactly being reasonable, but I was still annoyed that I had had to trek halfway across England like some tourist, following the huge map that Adira had held out not too embarrassingly across her face as if she had sight problems earlier on.

It had been nearly one hour before I had found the nearest train station, so I wasn't exactly feeling too cheerful or flexible. I was soaking wet as I had wrapped my rain coat around the diary, trying to prevent it from being damaged in any way. I mean, I was annoyed with Adira, but that didn't mean I was going to destroy the only thing I had that certified that I wasn't having hallucinations.

"Beryl! Are you even listening to me?" Why, god? Why does my real mother turn up when I was just getting used to the nice woman? I had just walked into the house, glad to see that the pink cloths had vanished from sight. I stepped onto the first step of the stairs only to hear a growl from behind.

My mother was standing right next to me with a terrifying expression on her face. It was so bad that I had nearly screamed before I realised that it was my mother scaring the crap out of me and not some hideous monster. I'd been grateful that it had been my mother at the time, but now I wished that it had been a monster.

"Beryl?" my mother asked me suddenly unsure of herself, her voice breaking at the end. That was when my mother buried her face in her hands and sat down heavily on the bottom step. I froze for a minute, not sure what to do. I felt like crying again. Seriously, I was turning into a living hosepipe.

"Mum?" When she didn't respond, I sat down next to her and put an arm around her shoulders. She started shaking, and it wasn't because she'd suddenly started dancing. She was *crying*. I had no idea what to do. I didn't know if I was supposed to pat her on the back and tell her that everything would be okay or go upstairs to my room and give her some privacy.

I was leaning towards option two, but that idea changed when I felt something wet drop onto my wrist. I glanced down and saw a perfectly clear jewel there. I was crying? Jeez, there must have been some sort of onion gas wafting around the building.

Strange sounds were coming from my mother. It sounded like she was trying to breathe, but she couldn't pull in enough air. That was hardly surprising, seeing as her hands were pressed to her face, and she was crying at the same time. I gently prised her hands away from her face, and, with second thoughts, twined my fingers in hers. She squeezed hard once.

"I didn't know if I'd lost you as well. I was stupid enough to let the love of my life go, and he was killed. I didn't want to lose my eldest daughter as well." My mother sobbed into her palms. I was flabbergasted. This was the first time Mum had brought my dad up in two whole months.

Typically, I wasn't exactly prepared. I leaned against the wall, and thought the way a soppy idiot would think. I thought about everything, thinking how I had lost nearly all the good things in my life. My friends and father weren't there for me anymore, my mother was losing the will to live, someone wants to kidnap me, and, most importantly, I was losing my sanity each day. Oh, and how could I forget? The world could end at any minute if this stupid Scroll of Elysium was stolen. My life had started to end as soon as I was told what I was abnormal.

I was about to stand up to go to my room and hang myself when I felt a small hand slip into mine. I opened my eyes to see my little sister holding mine and my mother's hands. She was crouching in front of me, her hair falling in front of her eyes.

"Mummy? Beryl? Why is Mummy crying?" Carla asked us, her hands still placed lightly in our grasps. Bless her, she was only four years old, and she had to go through the fact that her father was dead, and her mum and her older sister were freaking out (nearly) publicly.

That couldn't have put her at much of a social advantage, but she was at least still breathing and living. Sometimes, I love my family to bits, and, other times, I hate them like hell. My mother still didn't seem capable of forming coherent words, so I spoke instead. I didn't want Carla to think that we were mute as well. That might push her to consider committing suicide like me.

"We're fine, Carla. Everything's going to be all right. You'll see." I leaned towards my mother, pulled Carla close for a group hug and hugged them. I breathed in their familiar scents, feeling slightly comforted. I didn't miss the fact that I was trying to keep them all in one piece, and hugging them had been the simplest idea. At least it was easier than binding them together with rope and super glue.

I held them close for at least two minutes, feeling strengthened and hopeful, knowing that, whatever fate put in my life, my family would always be there to back me up. Maybe not Adrian, but you get the picture.

Great, now I sound like the one of those soppy losers at school that sit around in corners and cry because they're happy. I smiled at Carla who looked scared, as if she knew what was happening. I wish. Then it would be so much easier to explain to her (and my mum) why I was acting so strangely.

"Carla, go up to bed. I'll come up a bit later and read you a bedtime story." I certainly had a story to tell, but it wasn't your average bedtime story. It was a very unusual autobiography. Carla bounced up the stairs, crawling on her hands and knees while trying to get past my mum. Huh. No wonder people say that our family act more like animals than sane human beings. I'm not so surprised anymore.

I was about to follow her up and "chillax" upstairs, but a hand caught my leg from underneath, and I nearly fell headfirst to the stairs. Instead, I fell on my knees like I was begging.

"Phone Jill for me. I need to talk to her." I stared at her for a minute, not understanding who she was talking about. Had she finally lost her mind and thought that Carla was Jill? She looked sane enough.

"My sister Jill, your auntie." Oh, so that was who she was talking about. I was getting worried. When I still didn't respond, she pinched my leg hard with one hand. Yup, my real mother is back in town. And I don't think I'm going to enjoy her stay very much.

I got up smiling slightly but not too widely; like I said before, I want to live and grow old. I got Jill on the phone, and held it out to my mother who snatched it from my grasp without as much as a grunt of thanks. I like to know I'm appreciated once in a while.

I grinned to myself, only slightly, surprised by her wild mood swings. After all, I *did* grow up with her. If you were to meet her one day, you'd probably have the heart attack that I'm supposed to have.

As I walked up the stairs to read to Carla a story that I can guarantee she had never heard in her life, I laughed out loud. If there was an award for the strangest family, we would definitely win every year, and that's only if they knew half the story. The full one would blow their brains out their ears.

CHAPTER 7

"Wake up, sleepy head." I heard a soft voice say from up above. I smiled and rolled over on my bed thinking it was Carla. No, let me rephrase my sentence. I smiled and rolled over on my bed *wishing* it was Carla. Sadly, I have absolutely no luck stored up in the bank.

I groaned and buried my head under the pillow, only to have it yanked away from me like it didn't belong to me. I nearly threw up when I recognised the voice. It was the most evil, coldhearted *creature* I knew. No prizes for guessing who it was. It was—

"Beryl! Wake up for god's sake. You've got a busy day ahead of you, and you won't exactly be able to do anything while asleep." Adira poked me hard on the head. Oh why didn't I kill myself yesterday? I can't believe I actually thought everything was going to be all right yesterday. I have never been so wrong in my life.

I sat bolt upright, terrified that someone might walk into the room, like my *mother*. I couldn't imagine her taking that too lightly.

"Adira! What on earth are you doing here?" My whole family was almost definitely still in the house, and if my mother, at least, was not in the house, Carla wouldn't do anything short of phoning the police.

My mouth opened and closed like a goldfish out of water. I grabbed the brown bag in Adira's hand and held it close to my mouth in case I started hyperventilating. That's how scared I was. My family was no joke.

"Relax; your whole family are out on a family vacation for the rest of the day. I've got your whole day planned out. Your mother said it was fine if you spent the day out." Adira beamed like she was so proud of herself and that I should be smiling as well.

I practically growled at her, plucked the pillow from her fingers, and promptly tried to fall asleep again. I think Adira said something like "ok," but that couldn't have been possible. The next thing I knew, the room was shockingly quiet, and Adira wasn't in the room.

I sent up a thank-you prayer to heaven and sank headfirst into the pillow. I tucked the duvet tightly around my body and slept. At least, I tried to. I felt a sharp pain, and I suddenly found myself lying on my back.

"Wake up!" Adira yelled, and I felt water pouring onto my face from the bathroom jug. I spluttered and sat up, not wanting to drown in my bed. Adira was standing in front of me with some sort of horn thing that emitted the most annoying sound possible, the kind that drilled into your brain when you pressed.

"Well, it's not like you were going to wake up anytime soon by yourself," Adira said matter-of-factly, like she hadn't just wet my bed for me. Eww, that sounds wrong. I reached out and made out that I was going to yank the duvet that she had rolled at the end of the bed. All she did was throw it off the bed and onto the floor. I stared at her, furious.

"W-a-k-e-u-p," Adira sounded out. That was when I lost it.

"What the heck are you doing? This is my room, my house, and, most importantly, my bed, and I didn't let you in the house!" I screeched, not even caring that there might be a reason behind her throwing me out of my bed literally.

Adira had a look of shock drawn on her face. I stomped over to the bottom of my bed, grabbed my duvet, jumped onto the bed, and sank into bliss. At least, Adira had the sense not to try and stop me. I'm not exactly a morning person, and being wakened up with a cup of water thrown into my face had definitely gotten me out on the wrong side of bed.

I could feel someone's gaze on my face, and I slowly pulled the duvet away from my face. Adira was still staring at me with the same look of surprise etched on her face. If I wasn't feeling so tired and annoyed, I probably would have laughed by now.

"Not exactly a morning person, are you?" Adira said dryly, folding her arms across her chest while eying my bed head critically. I groaned and lay back.

"What do you want, Adira?" I asked wearily, all the anger drained from my voice. I wanted nothing more than to curl up on my bed and sleep for the next one hundred years like Sleeping Beauty. Some people just get all the luck. Adira instantly looked animated as I gave her the chance to explain herself without tearing out her throat.

"Well, you know how I was supposed to take you to Pelesmia last week, but it got late after everything that happened." I nodded cautiously. "Well, I thought I'd take you today!" she said brightly. I felt a spark of excitement, which was immediately dampened when

I remembered how she left me in the shack by myself, not knowing where on earth I was. I could have been in Albania for all I knew.

Well, no way was I going to have to go through that all over again. That is exactly what I said to her. Only I didn't tell her why. I was afraid I'd hit her and have to remember my traumatic experience if I did.

"Why not? It's gonna be fun." Adira looked so innocent and sweet that it was hard to imagine that she was so bad. I closed my eyes so I wouldn't have to see her angelic expression. For a second, I desperately wanted to do whatever she wanted me to do. I actually half-got up from the bed before tripping over my blanket and falling headfirst onto the floor.

I stared up at Adira accusingly. She had tried to do her freaky voodoo thing on *me* of all people. Without a word, I walked to my bed, not even sparing a glance for Adira. Like a young child having a fight for the first time, I pulled the duvet over my head. Don't get me wrong, I'm not inexperienced in fighting; I've had my share of fights, but, somehow, they were never like this.

"Go away now, please." When I heard a rush of air from next to me, I felt relief like I had never felt it before. Finally, my stalker had left me alone to let me live. I nestled into the bed and worried about what I was going to do about my mother, bro, and sis who were all apparently under the impression that they were all taking a family holiday.

All thoughts flew from my head as I began sweating under the covers. Whew! I'm sorry, but it's boiling hot under a thick winter duvet cover, and I felt claustrophobic. I waited for about five more seconds to make sure that Adira really *had* gone, and then I surfaced as if I was one of the passengers from the Titanic.

I blinked, waiting for my eyes to adjust enough to make out my surroundings. I smiled in bliss when I saw that the room was empty, and there was no one holding guard with a cup of water or a gun.

"Sorry," I started as a voice piped up from my left. Adira was perched comfortably on my rocking chair as if she had been there the whole time I was suffocating in my bed. Knowing her, she probably *had* been there. How thoughtful.

Before I could throw her out of my room (literally), she hurried on in her explanation of why she was not running away from me for her life. Trust me, in the mornings, I am not what you would call a pretty face, and seeing as I was not in a good mood, I probably resembled a zombie fresh from the grave.

"I'm really sorry, Beryl. I didn't mean to do that." I gave her a pointed glance. "Well, not really. But you know how it feels when you can't control what you're doing. So . . . please?" This time, it was my turn to flush. She did have a point, although when I'd read her mind, she'd nearly given me brain damage.

It's only fair I do the same thing to her. It was a bit too obvious what she would do to me if I ever tried to do that to her though—box my ears and then throw me out the nearest window. They should put her up as an attraction at Thorpe Park. She'd be an instant hit.

I looked at her grudgingly. I might as well forgive her. Plus it wasn't like I would be seeing much after I told her what I'd been thinking about for practically the whole night. I inadvertently glanced at Aya's diary and thought what she would do if she was in my position—the exact opposite of what I was about to do, if her diary gave me any clue as to the type of person she was.

"Yeah, yeah, whatevs. I forgive you." I said offhandedly. I was decidedly feeling guilty now about what I was going to have to do. Adira was babbling away mindlessly about what we were going to do today. Crap. If only she knew how much of that I would be missing out on.

Well, now was the time to end the nonsense! I wish I was as brave as that sounded. Unfortunately, that would never happen when it came to dealing with Adira. God, I sounded like a mother now. Only the good lord knows how on earth Adira's mother dealt with her. I feel sorry for her, even though she's dead. She'd probably roll over in her grave if she heard what Adira was now.

"Hey. Stop talking for a second. I have a mouth as well." I let out a nervous giggle that didn't fool her even the tiniest bit. If anything, it made her even more suspicious. She turned to face me, and the words I was about to say were lodged in my throat. I tried to clear it, but it wouldn't budge. I gave up.

"What? Spit it out." I wish. She had no idea how tight the little hairball in my throat was stuck. It was not comfortable. Thank god Adira can't read people minds like some freaks in this world. I looked hard at Adira (my mental barriers were up strong and high) and saw that, under her tough girl armour, she was just as nervous as me as she waited for what I would soon say.

The blocking in my throat cleared, my brain disconnected itself from my body, and my huge mouth opened and started blabbering like the idiot I was.

"I don't want to be a psychic mind reader any more. I give up. It's too hard, and I want to live a normal life again. I don't want to be a freak." I knew I sounded like a complete and utter coward, but it was true. I wanted to live a normal teenager life, complete with bossy parents (parent), annoying siblings, and fights with your girlfriends every other week.

I suddenly felt jealous of my ex-best friends, so fierce that I nearly fell down, and I wasn't even standing. I was still curled up on my bed. For a second, I wished I was JJ or Tamara or any other person on this planet who wasn't related to Aya.

Adira leaned over, and I thought for a second that she was going to hug me and tell me that everything was going to be all right. Obviously, I was completely and utterly wrong. She poked me hard on the chest, and I nearly fell back onto the brass bed frame.

"Why are you doing this?" She hissed to my face. "You want to be a normal stinking person? You get what you want. I don't need clumsy-minded people lumbering behind me like a freaks arcade. I can do this by myself. If I ever need help, I sure wouldn't come to you. And one more thing, just because I've left doesn't mean your 'powers' will go away!" Adira stormed. She flew out of the room as if she had some extra flying powers that she hadn't told me about before. Then it suddenly went all quiet, and what she was said suddenly hit me like a slap in the face.

Ouch. That stung. Did she just call me a groupie? I sat there in fury, not realising exactly what I had brought upon myself until about two minutes later. The full impact of what I had done hit me like a slap in the face.

I had just turned away from every single person who understood and accepted me for who I am. Now, I would have to live a boringly normal life while knowing that I could have lived the life of a superhero. What is wrong with me?

* * *

"Beryl, I want to buy some chocolate." Oh my god, I never thought in my whole life that the sound of any toddler's voice could sound as annoying as Carla's voice. Now, I was absolutely certain of that little fact. Sadly, the job of picking up Carla from school had been lugged onto my back ever since I hit my teens, and my mother couldn't be bothered to pick her up. If I didn't, Carla would probably live in the school. I don't even think anyone in the house would notice until they realise that no one was eating from Carla's plate.

"No. Carla, for the last time, you're not allowed! Remember the last time I gave you the crisps that JJ gave me, and you couldn't eat food for the rest of the day? Mum nearly hit me on the head with the frying pan." I'm not even exaggerating; my mother had chased me around the house, saying that one day I was going to kill her kids.

That seemed a little hypocritical to me seeing as she *was* the one running after me with a frying pan. If you ask me, that was a little over-reactive. I mean, it wasn't like the crisps were poisoned, and JJ and her mother were murderers in disguise, out to get us.

"Please? Pretty please, with sugar on top?" Carla pleaded, trying to do her little act of puppy dog eyes and looking up at me from under her lashes. No way was I going to fall for her act. That's how she gets most of the stuff that a normal five-year-old wouldn't get.

Well, I've had more than enough of Carla's sweet girl act. Though you have to admit, she *is* really sweet and cute when she wants to be.

I was just about to tell her that there wasn't a hope in hell of me budging when an old, homeless man sitting at the corner of the street caught my attention. He didn't look special in any way—on the contrary, he looked the way you would expect a homeless person look, you know, layers of clothing, a general feeling of unkemptness, and the look of a person who hasn't showered for a while.

What caught my eye wasn't the way he looked, but the cardboard sign that he was holding. Written on it in large, sprawling letters were the words: "Accept who you are for who you are, and don't try to hide what cannot be hidden. Be proud of what you are, and don't hide the qualities within you that other people do not judge as a good thing."

The man reminded me, strangely enough, of Morgan Freeman, I think his name was that. Ironic really, cause he was an old beggar in some film. I forgot what it was called though.

I walked as if I was in a daze to stand in front of the man but not close enough to be in his personal space. The man appeared to be sleeping, but he woke up when Carla bounded up to me, grabbed my hand, and made as if to pull me away from the man.

"Beryl, what are you doing?" It struck me as slightly funny that she sounded scared. A quick glance into her mind told me that she thought that this man was a drug dealer, and that he had messed up my mind with laughing gas. I almost snorted out loud. She had clearly been reading one too many Sherlock Holmes stories, even though I'm pretty sure she can't read.

I didn't say anything; I just gripped her hand tighter and squeezed it. I gazed into the man's bottomless, black eyes and was just about to ask him how he knew what I'd done when I felt myself being sucked into his eyes, knowing that I was doomed to fall forever. I screamed an endless yell, knowing that nobody could hear me . . .

I sat up straight in my bed, panting as if I had run the Olympics 4000-meter race. I was sweating all over, and the duvet was tangled around my body, making me feel trapped and suffocated. I couldn't help but feel relieved that it had all just been a dream, and I wasn't doomed for all eternity and falling through a never ending black hole. I concentrated on taking deep breaths in, and out, in, and out, repeatedly telling myself that it had all just been a silly dream.

It took me a full second to remember what the first part of my dream had been about. Instead of panicking about it or just simply pretending that it had never happened, I felt an unnatural calm settle over me like an English fog. I knew exactly what I had to do.

I threw my legs over the side of the bed, blinking the pulsing flashes of light away from my eyes. I stood in the dark, swaying with dizziness in the darkness, waiting for my eyes to adjust.

At times like these, I seriously wish I was a cat or one of those animals that can see in the dark. To save the trip of visiting Harry Potter at Hogwarts, I could have just eaten those carrots that my mother used to serve every day at dinner, which always used to somehow end up being flushed down the toilets. Thank god she never figured out why the pipes were always blocked. If she had, I wouldn't have been around to tell the tale.

I stood in the dark, leaning on the bedposts. I looked around the room, desperately hoping that that old man would pop into existence and tell me what the hell that dream had been all about. I mean, it was so vivid that I wouldn't be surprised if it was some messed-up vision.

I would have thought that, but it just didn't really . . . feel like one. It's like . . . when I have a vision, I get this *feeling*. Plus I always smell this really strong incense that's so strong that it nearly burns my nose off, and I couldn't smell anything this time round.

Now that I think about it, I haven't read any person's mind for the past week or had any visions recently. I haven't even thought about reading minds ever since I told Adira that I wanted to be a normal teenager; my mental barriers have been up for so long that I'm pretty sure that they're even up while I'm sleeping, even though I can't exactly check.

I wouldn't exactly be surprised if I found out that I couldn't pull the barriers down. I can't really help where and when I have my visions, so it's probably normal not to have a vision for a long amount of time. I hope.

Wait. What if Adira was wrong? And that it is possible to lose your . . . abilities if you don't use them for a long time? What if I was merely a *normal* person with nothing to differentiate from the rest of the billions of people around the world? That got me worried, which didn't make sense, seeing as, barely a week ago, I wanted to have no powers and live a normal, crappy life.

I must have been out of my mind. I'd rather be in the same room as Adrian and Carla for a whole day instead of being me on earth. Seriously? The one time I want a relative to test my skills on, is the one time my whole family was lying half dead on their beds, which is exactly where I want to be now.

I was getting desperate now, and I wanted nothing more than to fall back onto my bed and sleep. Sadly, that just wasn't possible as I'm like a goldfish. You know, a two minute memory doesn't remember a thing. Well, that's me when it comes to dreams. I forget them quicker than you can say the word "forgetful." It runs in the family.

Just as I was thinking about *family*, my eyes rested on Aya's diary. I hadn't had a chance to return it, seeing as Adira had nearly beaten me up and then jumped out of the window. It rested casually open on top of my drawers. I walked curiously towards it, sure that I had put it on my bookshelf behind the other millions of books piled there (I'm a serious bookaholic.)

There was a faint blue light emitted by it, giving the room a tint of blue, which I hadn't noticed before. I paused and pinched myself hard in the arm with my nails to make sure that this wasn't some freaky nightmare like in that movie, *Inception*.

Ow. That seriously stung though; I might as well have grabbed a knife and stuck it in my arm. That's how hard I pinch. Trust me on this; you would not want to be my brother or sister—get on my nerves and you would be purple and blue for the rest of your life. And it won't be from paint.

I stood in front of the book squeezing my eyes tightly shut, not wanting to see what was on the page. You would do the exact same thing if you were me. Imagine you buried a book under god knows how many books, making sure that no one would be able to find it, let alone you.

You then wake up in the middle of the night after having the strangest dream in the history of hallucinations to find the legendary book lying open and glowing blue right in front of your bed. Any sane person wouldn't think that everything was bumpety-bumpety fine unless they had some serious mental problems.

I half opened my eyes so that I could see the book but not clearly, seeing as my lashes were still locked together with chains and a bolt. To my surprise, there didn't seem to be anything written on the pages. It was just a blank, yellowed piece of parchment near the middle of the book.

I opened my eyes fully to see that the book wasn't glowing that weird colour anymore. I rubbed my eyes hard with my knuckles and opened my eyes again. It still looked the same as the last time I looked at it.

Uh-oh, I knew I was bound to go crazy one day or another, but I just didn't expect it to be in the middle of the night after some nightmare. I was just convincing myself that I was just imagining things and that books don't just start glowing in the dark randomly in the middle of the night when the pages rustled in the nonexistent wind.

I turned around to check that the windows were closed as tight as possible. They were, and I closed the door to make sure that there was no trace of wind left in the room. I never do that, as I hate being in closed spaces, and I wouldn't be surprised if I was claustrophobic.

The pages were still blowing gently, and I had the strangest feeling that I wasn't alone. Almost like something unnatural was in the room with me. I knew we never should have bought this house. Why didn't Mum listen to me when I told her this house was haunted?

Of course, it didn't exactly help that I was completely and utterly obsessed with horror books and couldn't go from one place to another without (apparently) seeing at least five ghosts. I wouldn't have been surprised if a ghost walked out of the wall and said that he was some long lost relative of mine.

Suddenly, out of nowhere, the book slammed shut, and I literally had to clap my hands over my mouth to keep from screaming aloud and causing my mother to phone the police. I stared at the diary, which had looked so normal just the day before, not able to move a muscle even if I'd wanted to.

When the book simply lay there, closed, I pinched myself lightly, enough so that I could go back to bed and convince myself in the morning that this had all been some messed-up dream. There was only one slight problem with that. Everybody within a thirty-mile radius including me knew that I just wasn't creative enough to come up with that all by myself.

There were only two options; Number one: I was crazy and having hallucinations. Number two: I've been watching way too many sci-fi movies. Well, the only way to solve my problem was to pretend it never happened. Anyway, like I said before, I have a two-minute memory, so it was most likely that I would forget everything before I got the chance to tell anyone.

I stood there in front of the journal for about ten minutes, motionlessly waiting for *something* that would tell me what the hell had just happened. The book lay there limp and dead with no sign of unnaturalness on it. It could have been any old book.

I sighed and walked lifelessly towards my bed, mentally vowing that I would wake up every hour to make sure that everything was where it should be, and there were no voodoo things flying around my room. All thoughts flew from my head as I sank into my still-warm bed, closing my eyes blissfully. I barely had time to pull the covers up and over my head before sleep dragged me down into its depth. And I have to say, I'm not complaining, at all.

*   *   *

I yawned and stretched, rolling my shoulders and rubbing my eyes. The house seemed unusually quiet, so that probably meant Mum and Carla had already left for school, and Adrian was god knows where. He could be on the streets drunk, and it was just as likely that he could be at the library, studying for his A-levels. I know which of the two was most likely.

I wondered half-mindedly (if that's even a word) why the windows and the door were bolted and locked. That was when everything came rushing back at me, so fast that I gasped aloud. I sat up straight and looked over the bedpost at my chest of drawers, wishing with all my heart that it was still closed.

Unfortunately, no one was there to hear my begging. The book lay open at a page near the end, but look on the bright side! It wasn't glowing blue anymore! No need to visit the optometrist. The last ten appointments had probably cost my mother the amount of money it would take to buy a car. No joke.

I gazed open-mouthed at the book, not believing what I was seeing. Dang, this had to be the one thing I didn't forget. And it wasn't a good thing.

I slowly put my legs, one by one, over the bed and onto the floor, taking the extra amount of time to put my furry animal slippers on and fold my bed. I actually considered going and having a shower and eating breakfast and everything, but, unfortunately, I was on the verge of exploding from curiosity.

I sighed and slowly made my way towards the diary. I picked it up carefully, making sure the page that it was open at was left open. I held my breath and looked down, fearing the worst. If my father's dead body popped into existence and said that he was back to destroy the world, I think I would actually be relieved. That would at least be easier to handle than what I was thinking.

Sadly, I have to prepare myself once in a while for disappointment, seeing as the odds were I was wrong. I was right to think like that as the page didn't have anything unusual written on it. In fact, it had absolutely nothing on it—pfft, so much for a dramatic ending.

I stared at the journal that lay so limply in my hands, disappointed beyond measure. I would have laughed at myself if I hadn't known the reason I was standing in the middle of the room practically crying over a piece of paper. I was about to throw the diary down back to where it came from (a forest on the other side of the world) when I noticed curling handwriting written at the top of the page.

I closed my eyes and opened them again, sure to the point that I would have bet my life on it that the writing hadn't been there when I first picked it up. I opened my eyes, and the writing was still there as surely as my name was Beryl. I leaned closer towards the book to read the minuscule writing. It read:

Write what you may

And we shall obey.

I stared blankly at the sheaf of parchment that seemed to yell my name for what must have been a couple of hours. At least, it felt like that. I glanced around the room, checking that everything was where it should be, and there was nothing flying around the room trying to kill me. I'm not even joking.

I walked over towards my bed, went down on my hands and knees (not to pray, even though that seemed like a logical thing to do), and scooted around under my bed for a pen with one hand. Trust me on this, you would *not* want to go rummaging around on the floor under my bed—it's not exactly what I would call clean.

Little dust bunnies floated out from under my bed and wafted into my nose as if my nose holes had a string pulling them towards me. I sneezed hard, and it wasn't one of those dainty, little girly sneezes. It was one of those mad, out of control snorting sneezes, which caused me to jump half a foot into the air.

Of course, it would have been all right if I was standing, but, unfortunately, I was under a bed with my arm stuck out in front of me like a blind man reaching for his cane. I banged my head against the bottom of the bed, and it didn't really help that my bed was made out of metal.

Little stars and rockets were zooming in front of my eyes, and I fell flat on my face on the ground groaning in pain. Jeez, how hard is it for a perfectly able person to get a pen from under her bed. Seeing as this is me we are talking about, it was almost like mission impossible, only without the superpowers.

I hoisted myself on my elbows and shuffled backwards, bottom first, out from under the bed, grabbing the pen that was just within my reach.

I stood up, almost passing out from the sharp pain that lashed through my head from the sudden movement. I gingerly felt the back of my head, and I could feel a massive bump the size of an egg sitting like it belonged there. Well, it most certainly did not. I was about to run down the stairs and get an ice pack to put on my head when I remembered the diary still lying open on top of my drawers.

I couldn't think whether or not the words written on the page would disappear as soon as I left the room. I stood there for at least five minutes, arguing with myself and occasionally taking a step closer to the door. The throbbing at the back of my head was becoming more and more painful as I stood there, and, eventually, the pain pushed me over the edge.

I ran out of the room and down the stairs as fast as I could, without falling over for once in my stupid life, yanked the freezer door open, grabbed the ice pack, and ran back up the stairs. I did all of this so fast that it would make Usain Bolt look slow as a snail—in my opinion.

The diary was still lying open as if it had been waiting for me all its life. I stared cautiously at the book like I was scared that a lion was suddenly going to pop out of nowhere and eat me. Knowing how life really was, that would probably be considered normal in Peles whatnot.

Why can't I just go back to the normal life I used to lead? Well, as close to normal as I can get. I pulled together all of my strength and forced my suddenly motionless legs into action.

I stood in front of the diary, reading and rereading the words written so casually on the page. I suddenly felt this weird inner peace thingie magige inside of me. Great, now I sound the way a psychic is supposed to sound. Amazing; all I have to do is dress like a gypsy now, and I'll be perfect.

Anyway, I felt all calm and peaceful, like I had been meditating a hundred years. I'm telling you, it wasn't at all natural what I was feeling. Of course, psychics aren't what I would call normal, but you get the picture. I'd never felt anything like it before.

I would have had a panic attack if I wasn't feeling so annoyingly calm. It was almost annoying if I wasn't feeling so ladida and not in a good way. I glanced down at my hand which was the only sign that showed everything wasn't okay. It was clenched into a tight fist around my pen that seemed to be squealing for mercy—literally. I slowly unclenched my hand and placed the pen gently onto the smooth wood that seemed to caress the diary.

I picked up the pen again and stared at it. It occurred to me how stupid I was being. I was scared to write in a diary of all things? I mean, sure, it had been glowing in the middle of the night. And, yeah, it had popped out from behind my cupboard like some freaky magicians trick that had gone completely and utterly wrong. But, all in all, it was still a journal that an old lady liked to write in.

I was simply making a huge deal out of everything, the way I always did. I felt like kicking myself. I felt something remarkably like anger flash inside of me, which couldn't have been possible because I was still feeling really nice and calm.

I yanked the pen up from the desk, and was about to jam the nib of the pen into the page, when I felt . . . hesitant. I just couldn't bring myself to write on the pristine page. That's it. I am officially going to join Sissies Anonymous. I would fit in perfectly.

I stared at the gathering little ball of ink on the tip of my pen. It steadily grew larger and larger until it dropped delicately onto the page. I held my breath and waited. The ink sat there, quivering for a while, and then it sunk smoothly into the page until it completely vanished. My mouth plopped open, and my icepack fell limply from my hand to hit the floor with a dull thud.

I couldn't believe what I had just seen. I mean, ink doesn't vanish on a daily basis if at all. I rubbed my eyes hard, almost blinding myself in the process. I opened my eyes, and the page had no more writing on it than it had had five minutes ago. I felt like clawing my eyes out; that's how useless they felt.

Instead of running away screaming the way a normal girl would, I looked at the page again and reread the words. They seemed to have a different meaning now that I wasn't scared rigid.

I closed my eyes and thought hard about what I most wanted. Aside from the obvious (you know, win the lottery every time round or make every person worship the ground I stepped on), there wasn't much that I actually wanted.

I stared down at the book blindly, unsure of what to do next. I mean, what type of person would make a wishing page in the middle of their diary? That just wasn't possible, a wishing page in the middle of a diary—strange.

The shock of realisation hit me like a ton of bricks. You could say that I had been enlightened. *I wanted to be a freak,* seriously. And that's not the end of the torture. *I didn't even care what other people thought of me.* To be honest, I never really cared what other people thought of me; but, now that I actually knew what they were thinking, that changed things—a lot.

But really, I wanted to be a mind reader, and, like Adira had so very kindly mentioned, it wasn't like my *powers* were about to go away any time soon. I looked down at the clear page and knew exactly what I had to do.

I picked the pen up slowly but surely, placed the tip of it on the page, and began to write.

Find me a way to speak to Adira. I wrote out the words large and clear, so the words couldn't be mistaken for anything else. Even though I knew what I was asking for was near impossible, it was worth giving a shot. You can't know until you try.

I held my breath and waited, crossing my fingers without realising it behind my back. The silence in the room was almost suffocating, and I could feel my palms sweating as I waited for the diary to do something.

The page seemed to ripple like water as the words sunk down into the page, just like the ink blob had done not too long ago. My hand flew to my neck, and I stifled a gasp through my fingers, which had somehow wrapped itself around my face. I held my breath, waiting for something to happen.

It became apparent that nothing especially amazing was going to happen anytime soon. I frantically scanned the page, praying (Ironic really) for anything to happen. At that point, I would have been happier if a horde of stampeding elephants came stamping out of the page than if nothing was to happen. At least, that would prove that I wasn't completely insane.

Just as I was beginning to lose hope of ever being able to call myself sane, I noticed a small block of light slowly getting bigger at the corner of the page. It soon became evident that the square wasn't about to stop growing any time soon. I let my breath out in a noisy gush of air and rested my butt against the corner of the desk. I glanced over at the diary like every second, my eyes flicking back and forth from the clock hanging on my bedroom. Was it just my imagination, or was the clock ticking by slower than usual?

After what felt like a couple of years, I glanced at the diary for what I hoped would be the last time. Thank god I was right. I was seriously considering tearing my hair out. What had once been a little square of light was now some sort of television. Through it, I could see a dark-skinned girl with braided hair that covered her face, so I couldn't really identify who the African queen was.

She was sitting cross legged on a massive metal bed with the most delicate, curling roses on the edges. It was exactly what I would expect to see in Buckingham Palace. Believe me; you would get exactly what I was talking about if you were in here with me.

While I was gawping at the bed like the idiot I was known to be, the girl on the bed raised her head and looked straight at me. I felt a chill run through my spine as I finally realised why the girl sitting on the bed looked so familiar. It was Adira.

Chapter 8

"Beryl?" Adira sounded too surprised to throw the pen that was in her hand into my eyes. All I can say to that is thank god. Whenever I even thought about talking to Adira face to face, all I had been able to think of was six-eyed monsters trying to rip my throat out. Her reaction wasn't exactly what I had thought it would be. For one thing, she hadn't attempted to try and kill me yet, so that, at least, was a good thing.

Adira's face was actually quite comical now that I think about it; her eyes were bulging the way Tom and Jerry's eyes pop out in like every episode, and her mouth was hanging open like all the muscles in her cheeks and mouth had suddenly stopped working. Judging from her reaction, I would say that the odds of her being able to see me were quite high.

"Um . . . hi?" I raised my arm half heartedly at a feeble attempt to wave. I flushed when Adira continued to stare at me like she didn't know who the hell I was. I'm not saying that it would be a bad thing if she forgot who I was—it would save me having to go and buy armour. Adira opened her mouth as if to say something. And it wasn't a loving declaration of how my missing friendship had left her brokenhearted. In fact, it looked more like she'd prefer tearing my heart from my chest and breaking it.

"What are you doing here?" It was more of a statement than a question. And boy did she look scary. If I had the choice to choose whether to fight Adira or an army of vampires, I know which one I'd choose.

"Well, er, I'm really sorry about saying all that bullpoopie about wanting to be a normal person 'cause, to tell the truth, it sucks." I held my breath, waiting for Adira to say something. To my surprise (and relief), her face broke out into a welcoming smile, and she looked as if she was going to start singing.

I felt this warm little glow inside my heart, and my face broke out into a smile. You had to give it to Adira. I had put her through hell, and she still put up with me. At least, I hope she will.

A noise made me zap myself out of my daydream. Adira had started laughing hysterically like she had suddenly gone high or drunk. I stared incredulously at her. This was *so* not how I had imagined we would meet. It was more of a catfight that I had envisioned. I waited as patiently as I could for Adira to stop screeching like a witch.

"Are you serious? You honestly think I'm going to forgive you that easily?" Adira snorted, folding her arms contemptuously across her chest. Oh. Ok. Forget everything I said about Adira being an understanding person because I was completely wrong about that.

Sadly, all I had left to do was grovel and beg. Ugh. That is *so* not my style. Oh well, might as well try my best at begging. I ought to be an expert on begging, seeing the way I was brought up.

I threw, myself onto the floor, and clasped my hands in front of my chest as if I was praying. From Adira's horrified expression, I could tell that even though I was on the floor, she could still see me clearly.

"Please, I'm begging you. I don't want to be a normal boring human anymore. I was a stupid cow, and all I'm asking is for you to enlighten me with the knowledge of your power." Okay. Maybe that was a *little* too dramatic, but it seemed to be working. I raised my head just a little bit to try and see her expression.

Her mouth had once again swung open so I could see her perfect rows of teeth. Great, why is it that only some people have to be so perfect when there are people who look like me out on the streets?

Her eyes were unreadable, and I didn't even try to hide the fact that I was staring at her with a stupid glimmer of hope in my eyes, like all my happiness depended on what she said. She appeared to be thinking hard, and I waited with bated breath. She finally opened her mouth to speak after what felt like two hours had passed. To my surprise, she sounded a little haughty.

"There wasn't really any point in you begging me like some bad rerun of the *Simpsons*. I was only pulling your leg. Part of being the royal scribe to the Wrayalis means that if we happen to find a gifted human, we have to help and guide them in mastering their strength." She paused to look up at the ceiling as if asking for help and rolled her eyes. "We're bound by law."

Huh. Well, thank you very much for telling me that. Only problem was that I'd already gone and made a fool of myself by begging. I got up disgruntled and stared down at the diary, wishing that a hole would pop up somewhere in the ground that I could sink into.

"Well, thanks for telling me that. I'll just mind my own business and stay where I'm supposed to." I said sweetly, making gestures that showed I was going to slam the book shut. Adira, once realising what I was planning to do, stood up and walked closer to the screen.

"Do not close the book." She said in the same commanding voice that she had used on my mother so long ago. Quick as a flash, I threw my mental barriers up stronger than ever and watched Adira's expression change into one of surprise and guilt. Seeing as I was a sweet and loving person, I decided to let that little offence pass by. After all, I *had* done worse things.

"Why shouldn't I?" I said in that same annoying voice. Adira *had* to be getting desperate now. Sure enough, her wide brown eyes looked a little larger than usual.

"Think about it. If you turn away, you'll have nothing left to look forward to everyday other than thinking about why you missed out on a great opportunity just because you had a fight with some person." Adira must have seen me hesitate as she grabbed at the chance to convince me even more.

"You know what? Why don't you come over to Pelesmia today, and I can show you what you'd be missing out on. If you still want to be mortal, it's your choice." Adira waited expectantly for me to tell her whether it was a deal or a no deal.

It *was* the best offer that I could have gotten, and it was better than what I had been hoping for. Yet there was a small part of me that was telling me that going to Pelesmia was a seriously bad idea. But what could actually happen to me on a harmless outing with a "friend"? I mean, I know it isn't your average trip but still. Abandoning all the sanity that I still had, I nodded vigorously.

"Great! You can come over now." She took a step back as if she was making some space for me. Clearly, I wasn't the only person who had lost her mind.

"Uh, how exactly am I supposed to do that? And don't expect me to go that old house again because I most certainly am not going all the way there," I said. This was, at least, one thing that I was 100% sure of.

She stared at me as if the answer was right in front of my face. When I stared blankly back at her, she sighed as if she was a tutor for a mentally disabled child.

"In case you haven't noticed, the only reason that I am standing here talking to you from Pelesmia is because we are talking through a portal."

"A what?" Adira rolled her eyes again, and I could swear that she muttered under her breath, "humans these days." Huh. Well, she can't chat, seeing as she used to be a human way before my time—old women these days.

"A portal is basically a sort of seeing glass that enables people to talk to each other. How you managed to make one without even knowing what you were doing is something only god knows."

I glared at her, more annoyed at myself than her. I mean, what type of idiot would make something without even knowing what they were doing? I mean, sure, I knew that I wanted to speak to Adira, but I was thinking that a telephone would be more appropriate. I hadn't really expected to talk to Adira face to face. That was just a tad out of my league.

"Okay smartass, you know what a portal is, but what you haven't told me is how I'm going to get from my bedroom in England to your bedroom all the way in Pelesmia." Instead of Adira looking like a lost gorilla in the middle of Hyde Park, she looked like she knew the answer to my question. Don't get me wrong, I think I know how to do it, but I'm pretty sure that I'm wrong.

"Stick your hand through the book. Your whole body should be sucked through the portal and into my room." Adira paused, evidently enjoying the fear that had to be flicking across my face— evil old woman.

I stretched my arm out cautiously over the diary and held it there for a couple of seconds. I just couldn't bring myself to do it. What if my arm was the only thing that went through the portal and the rest of my body stayed back in England? That can't be too comfy.

I glanced up at Adira and saw that her face was a mixture of mock and trepidation. That put an end to my doubts. If there was anything that I hated more than people who make weird noises when they eat, it was being laughed at.

If you told me to jump off a cliff then called me a chicken for not doing it, I would probably take my coat and shoes off and throw myself of the cliff. Either that or I'd commit suicide, by jumping off the same cliff.

I took a deep breath in, closed my eyes so I didn't have to see Adira's face, and plunged my arm into the book. It was just like the movies; I could feel my body being sucked into the book quicker than you could say, "Blackberry's suck." I'm not even joking.

I could hear wind rushing past my ears, and what sounded alarmingly like a million other voices drifting in and out from my hearing.

Before I could open my eyes, everything went still and I could smell some sort of sweet incense that wafted under my nose, tempting me. I opened my eyes to see Adira standing in front of me, twisting her hair round and round her finger anxiously. My vision wavered for a second, and I was hit with the worst bout of dizziness that I had ever experienced. My stomach rolled alarmingly like I was about to throw up.

"I made it," I said in a voice barely audible. Then I fainted clean away.

*   *   *

"Beryl, Beryl, Wake up," an insistent voice repeated over and over again until I could bear it no longer. I opened my eyes to tell whoever it was to shut up and leave me alone when I was momentarily blinded by the bright lights shining in through the large square windows. I could feel something damp resting on my forehead, and, when I raised my hand to brush it away, I could feel that it was a wet towel.

"What-" I tried to get up, but brightly coloured bobbles were bouncing to and fro in my vision. Once my sight was clear, I turned my head to see Adira standing somewhat awkwardly next to the bed that I was perched on.

"I am really sorry. I didn't think that travelling through a portal would affect you the way that it did. It seems that portals aren't designed to transfer humans to other worlds." Adira tried to smile, but I could see guilt riddled in her clear brown eyes. "Here—drink this. It'll help. It's better than any of the human remedies."

I took the glass in my hands and stared down anxiously at the liquid inside that bubbled and throbbed gently. It was a pure gold colour that made my stomach squirm. I had never eaten or drunk anything with that colour. It looked like urine. It smelled surprisingly good though. I glanced up at Adira questioningly, but she was staring down at her polished blue toenails.

The drink wasn't going to get any tastier, so I might as well just drink it all in one go. I took a deep breath in and raised the vial up to my lips, taking in a huge sip. The taste of it was quite surprising— it tasted like a blend of apricots, mangos, and buttermilk. It was delicious. I had downed the whole cup before I knew it.

Instantly, I could feel the change in my body. For one thing, I actually felt like my brain and body were connected. I shook my head experimentally, and, sure enough, the world didn't turn upside down. I felt *great*.

"What is this stuff?" I asked. I felt like doing cartwheels round and round the room even though I knew I couldn't even do a cartwheel in the first place. I threw my legs over the edge of the bed and stood up, feeling like, if I sat on the bed for a second more, I would go mad.

"It's Ambrosia, nectar of the Gods. Of course, the Wrayalis are basically like God, so it's their creation." Adira looked like she was about to nibble her bottom lip off.

"Come on; loosen up for god's sake. It's not like you knew I was going to be sick. Besides, I feel absolutely great! It's a great day, and it's not going to be any fun if you're going to act like a great big dope all day."

I actually felt the way I'm guessing drunk people feel—you know, giddiness and unexplained happiness coming from out of nowhere. To my surprise (even in my drunken state), Adira smiled at me.

"That's it. No more Ambrosia for you. I'm learning and remembering more and more about being human." From the tone of her voice, I could tell that she didn't associate being human as a good thing. Oh well, I was really too high to really notice the symptoms of a bad mood coming along. Anyway, might as well enjoy the moment of being happy and carefree while I still had it.

I strode over to the door and opened it wide. I turned around and made movements with my hands to show that I was waiting for Adira to come follow me, and if she didn't, I would go right on without her. Plus if my information was correct, she was bound by law to help me. Shame on you Adira!

Jeez, the Ambrosia thingie magige had really gone to my head. I was acting worse than my mother on Christmas Eve whenever she drank too much wine. All I'm saying on that topic is that it isn't a very pretty sight. I hope to god that I didn't look anything like her.

Adira made no movement, so I took a step out of the room, not even joking. And I began to walk confidently down the hallway as if I knew where I was going. Pfft, like I knew what I was doing. I barely know the way to school, let alone some type of palace in the middle of an unknown world that wasn't in the Atlas.

I heard soft footsteps coming up from behind me until they were evenly paced with my steps. I smiled inside, knowing that they were Adira's. I was feeling hyper aware—I actually felt like I could see all the ants and bugs in the soil that lay outside in the bright sunshine.

I glanced over at Adira, and I could see that she was still wrapped up in her own little world of misery. I looked more closely at her, sensing that she was more upset than she was letting on. All traces of happiness vanished as she looked over at me, and I could clearly see that Adira was in more pain than Mums are when giving birth.

"What *are* you thinking about?" I half whispered, aware of how loud my voice sounded, echoing down the long marble corridor. We had reached the end of the hallway, and we were now walking down loads of long, twining stairs that spiralled downwards. Adira didn't say anything until we had gone down one flight of stairs.

"My past human life," Adira answered, looking down at the floor, not quite meeting my eyes, like she was scared that I was going to read her mind. Even though I was high, I would never do that when she was obviously feeling unsure of herself in her fragile state of mind. Great, now I sounded like a frickin' psychiatrist.

"Do you want to talk about it or . . ." My voice trailed off, unsure of what to say.

I thought Adira might give me a little credit for not bursting into her mind like a pompous policeman and reading it. If anyone tried to read my deepest secrets, I would probably bust the vein on the side of my head that I always get whenever I'm really stressed or angry.

Why do I have to be the one to have the power of invading people's privacy of their minds? While I was pondering the effects of being a criminal mastermind, Adira had stiffened beside me.

"No," Adira's voice blasted out from her body with the force of a bullet—so much for appreciation. I didn't say anything. Hurt was oozing through my body like syrup on pancakes, and I wasn't about to show that to her.

I looked straight ahead at what seemed to be a never ending staircase. Finally, the Eiffel Tower has some competition for the most number of steps.

I glanced over at Adira and saw that she looked as if she was about to cry. I was too surprised to look away and pretend that I hadn't seen her. She looked over at me and took a deep breath in.

"Sorry. As you can clearly see, my human life is a kinda sensitive subject for me, even though it was such a long time ago," Adira said, taking in one deep rattling breath and closing her eyes. When she opened them, they were once again peaceful and untroubled. By now, I was almost bursting with curiosity. What had happened to Adira that would turn her into a trembling wreck the second it was mentioned?

I desperately wanted to ask Adira, but I was afraid she'd do some more of that weird voodoo thing on me. Please, I'd had more than enough to do with unnatural stuff (the human definition of unnatural I mean).

"I guess you want to know what happened to me." Adira paused as if thinking hard. "To be honest, in a way, you have a right to know. It would help you in some ways."

I didn't need to read Adira's mind to know that she knew I had no idea what on earth she was talking about. If she was going to tell her story while speaking in riddles, she might as well not tell me. It'd be exactly the same. I didn't say anything. I just looked at her.

We were still walking, and I found that I was still able to concentrate on what she was saying and carry on walking. My legs were starting to ache like hell, and the stairs gave no sign of ending. Thank god we were going down the stairs—if we were going up, I'd have had a psychotic fit.

"Well, you already know that, when I was a normal human, I met what I thought was a good man." Adira paused, glancing over at me to see that I knew what she was talking about. She had told me this before when we had first met, but I don't see why this would make her so upset unless he raped her or something horrible like that.

"He told me his name was Nathanial. He was supposed to help me. This was about five years after I found out that I could control people. It was frightening to say the least. The first time I found out I could make people do things was when I was around ten years old. I had had a fight with a friend, and I told her to jump of the roof of the school and jump off into the pool underneath.

What I didn't know was that the bottom of the pool had layers of rocks underneath it for natural reasons. You can guess what happened." She winced as if she was there again. That must have been horrible to watch. Imagine watching one of your friends die, and it was all because of you. I would probably have had my foretold heart attack early.

"Well, anyway, I met Nathanial when I was fifteen. He told me that my parents had sent him to protect me, which was absolutely ridiculous; but, for my whole life, I had fantasized that my parents were watching out for me. They were dead you know. I was living in an orphanage at the time," she said matter-of-factly as if she was telling me what the weather was going to be like tomorrow.

You know, flat, expressionless tone of voice that makes you want to go and jump of a ship in the middle of the Pacific Ocean—I felt really bad for her though. I still had a mother, alive and kicking, even though, most of the time, I felt like killing her. I looked at Adira wordlessly, waiting for her to continue her fairytale, which didn't seem to have a happy ending. She was staring straight ahead, her eyes fixed on something that I couldn't see.

"He told me what I was, and what it was I could do. Obviously, I had no clue as to what the hell he was talking about, but I drank it all in. See, I was desperate to prove myself and make people know that I wasn't just some poor orphan kid with no family. I'd already had great grades and loads of friends, but it just wasn't enough. Nathanial"—she said the name with a wrinkle in her face as if she was sucking on a lemon—"seemed like the perfect opportunity to do just that. What I hadn't known was the uses that he would put me to." She chuckled darkly as if remembering some long forgotten joke.

"I began noticing how edgy he was acting. He had started asking me every time I went to see him questions like 'What did you dream about last night?' or 'Does this room look familiar?' I never understood why he was asking me these, and, whenever I asked him, he would laugh it off or something like that.

He always seemed as if he was hiding something big that I should have known about. Of course, if I had been you, I would have been able to find out straight away, but I couldn't exactly read minds. He had always told me that he was a descendant of Aya who wasn't gifted, but that didn't seem right. There was something about him that seemed off, and I got the feeling that even if I could read minds like you, it wouldn't work on him.

He started to tell me to do some seriously messed-up things. For one thing, they nearly always included pain, mostly self-inflicted. I began to listen to him more carefully than I had ever done before. Most of the stuff that he said, even perfectly harmless little things, nearly always had a double meaning.

It was when I was sixteen that I really saw him. I'll never forget that night. Sixteen is the age that most of the gifted descendant's powers would have developed to their full ability. I was showing no signs of being able to do anything other than control people, and this, apparently, wasn't good enough for Nathanial. He went mad.

I remember Nathanial not being the quiet and reserved person he usually was. He seemed on the edge of breaking apart. He told me to do things that I would never ever have thought of doing. He was practically telling me to kill people. I obviously refused. He just blew up like a dormant volcano.

He started calling me these horrible names that should never be spoken to a living creature. He threw things at me, anything that was within reaching distance. He kicked, pinched, and slapped me until I could feel the black and blue bruises forming on my skin.

He seemed to have had enough of hurting me, or he just got bored, and he finally stopped, only to pick up a piece of broken glass that was resting against the wall. He smiled widely, and that was the last thing I remember seeing. I closed my eyes, not wanting to see the way he planned my death because I knew the result would definitely be painful, and watching the smug look on his face as he watched me slowly die wouldn't exactly help.

I heard the sound of a heavy object swishing towards my head, and I braced myself for the pain that I knew was going to hit me. It didn't come though. I heard a loud thud and the sound of something heavy falling through the air. Once I had opened my eyes, I saw Nathanial lying motionless on the floor in front of me.

You could say that it scared the hell out of me, but this fear was deeper than the usual little jumps that I got. You already know that I meditated for seven years, living on only water, but the reason I told you wasn't true. I wasn't afraid to die. I mean, I was kinda scared, but it was the normal reaction that a human would get from death. I did what I did because I wanted to understand what had made Nathanial nearly kill me and what it was that he had been hiding from me.

I meditated for seven years, and, after that, I was . . . well, you could say that I was enlightened," she chuckled dryly. "I finally found out who Nathanial really was. You may already know about the tribe of Ironcia."

I nodded, feeling slightly smug at finally knowing something, even though I was fairly certain that it had been Adira who had told me about it. I couldn't really see what the point of telling me about the tribe of Ironcia was when she was in the middle of telling me her life story. Maybe she was going to rip her face off and tell me that she was the leader in disguise, and she had come to take me away. Anything was possible now. I probably wouldn't even be surprised.

"It turned out that Nathanial was the leader of Ironcia in human form, using a recently-passed-away human body. He had been helping because he had thought that I might be a psychic and help him," she said in a rush, almost as if she was embarrassed to say those words aloud.

They sounded oddly familiar to me. I racked my brains, trying to remember. *"It's your father's body . . ."* Holy crap, the spirit was coming for me as well, and if I don't do what it wants me to do, I would be dead meat—literally. And only god knows what they would do to my body once I died—nothing too good probably.

"Wait . . . you're saying that this Nathanial person nearly killed you because you aren't psychic? And I am? Jeez, what is he planning to do to me when I refuse to help him? Throw me in the Niagara

Falls?" Even as I joked weakly, a deep feeling of dread settled in my stomach.

I actually *did* have a death sentence after all, and, surprisingly enough, my mother wasn't the one to deal it out. The watery smile on my face clearly wasn't fooling Adira though as she smiled kindly at me for a change.

"Don't worry; you'll always be safe. There'll always be somebody there with you, whether it's me, your Erylenne, or even your Inlai, even if she does do nothing other than sit around in your belly and sleep." I could tell that Adira was doing her best to try and cheer me up, but I'm afraid she failed that little test. I still felt as if the spirit/Nathanial/leader of Ironcia was going to smash through all the windows of this place and chop my head off, the same way Henry VIII did to his wives, only with a lot more screaming.

I tried to subtly change the subject, but, of course, I was no actor. There was a reason why I fail my drama exams every year.

"Uh, how come these stairs are so long? Do they never end?" I asked, staring down at the marble stairs which showed no signs of ending—great. Way to go, Beryl. Ask-the-most-random-question award has just been won by . . . Beryl! To my surprise, Adira flashed a sheepish look at me, her mouth slightly upturned at the corners. I looked at her quizzically.

"Well, you see, these stairs are enchanted. It becomes as short or as long you want it to be. I asked to have it made like this because I like to walk around when I'm thinking or telling a story." Adira smiled at me sheepishly, and, even though I felt like killing her, I felt an answering smile spread across my face. I mean, how cool can this place get?

Even though, by that point, I was getting pretty excited about something as simple as a staircase, I still had a little bit of common sense left. I mean, I know that most normal people (make that all) wouldn't ever get a chance to walk on something as cool as it, but my legs were seriously aching by then. Plus Adira could easily make them stop. I didn't even have to say anything to her. The expression on my face must have tipped her off that I wasn't a very happy little birdie at that moment in time.

"I guess you want to stop walking now." I merely nodded once, and I could feel the floor flattening under my feet to make an even surface that I could walk on. At the end of what was now a hallway, there stood large, wooden double doors that had a rectangle glass on top of them. The daylight danced through the glass, making little diamonds on the smooth marble. I suddenly felt claustrophobic, and I sped up my walking and worked my tired legs harder.

I pushed the doors open and stood outside in the warm sunlight streaming down onto my body like a soft blanket wove by a loving mother. For a moment, I just stood there looking around.

I caught a brief glance of huge, old-fashioned buildings looming up from the ground before I was distracted by a scream from behind me. I turned around to see what had caused the scream when I felt something hard and very much solid smash into my back. I felt a moment of pure pain and fear. The floor slammed to meet me, and that was the last thing I could remember . . .

CHAPTER 9

"Beryl, wake up my sweetheart." That sweet voice was all that was needed to drag me out of my mini coma. I could feel a hand, light as a feather, gently holding my right hand. I opened my eyes thickly, unsure of where I was or even who I was with. I tensed myself for the pain that I knew was bound to come; but, to my surprise, nothing happened. Judging from the hard, gritty surface that I could feel under my thin shirt, I gathered that I was on lying on the ground.

There was utter silence that was broken by my heavy breathing that instantly felt uncomfortable. I pulled myself upright, once again surprised by how effortless that seemed. It was almost like I didn't even have a body; that's how light I felt. I leaned on my elbows, and looked around myself.

People were paused halfway through whatever it was they were doing. They seemed almost frozen to me. I would have bet that if I touched them, they would feel like ice under my touch. That is if I could even touch them. For all I knew, I could have been dead.

I looked down at myself, and I could see that whoever it was holding my hand still had me firmly in grasp. I slowly looked up the same way people did in the movies until my eyes came to rest on a young woman who looked only a couple of years older than me. She had flaming red curly hair that rested softly against her chest and back and bright eyes that were the colour of the Caribbean Sea and just as deep. Somehow, before she opened her mouth, I knew who she was. The woman standing (well, sitting) next to me was Aya.

I mouthed wordlessly at her like a fan who was finally meeting her favourite celeb. That was how pathetic I was acting. Once I had managed to pull myself together, I spluttered out incoherent words.

"You—you're . . . you're Aya!" I spluttered slightly hysterically as I tried to straighten out my breathing. Seriously? I might as well have thrown myself at her feet and declared my love for her. I should have figured it out straight away though. Wasn't freezing time what Aya was known for being able to do?

Aya waited patiently as she waited for me to find my sanity again. Even though this seemed highly unlikely, I appreciated the gesture. Once I had gotten my breathing under control, I looked at Aya, waiting for her to say something and act professional.

"Beryl, as much as I'd like to get to know you better, there is no time to waste. Every second is precious." Even as Aya spoke, I knew that something serious was going on. I knew I was being silly, but I couldn't help feeling a little hurt that Aya had ignored me for my whole life but turned up when there was a problem.

I tried to push down those feelings and focus on what she was saying to me. I mean, something must really be messed-up if she was bothered to come here from wherever it was that dead people went when they kicked the bucket.

"Beryl," she said my name again. I was tempted to tell her that I already knew that she knew my name, but something inside me was telling me that that would probably make Aya freeze *me* and smash me into little pieces.

"You may already know about the Tribe of Ironcia, and what it is that they are planning to do. They are planning to steal the Scroll of Elysium." Even though I had heard this said by two different people, it still gave me a chill to hear it being said so casually. Aya continued talking as if she hadn't noticed my reaction. We were both sitting cross legged on the hard, gritty surface of the ground.

"They have unfortunately found a way to get the Scroll of Elysium. Even as I speak, they are preparing to leave and seek out the legendary Scroll of Elysium. What I am now going to tell you must never be spoken to another living soul or even a spirit unless they need to know or you trust them with your life. I am trusting your judgement." As soon as I heard those words being spoken, I felt a jolt go down my spine; but, this time, it was from excitement. *I was about to be told something by my legendary grandma that was such big news that I couldn't tell anyone else.*

Admit it. If it were you, you would be jumping up and down and singing nursery rhymes. Thankfully, I am not you, so I just sat very still on the ground like a good little girl. All I had to do now was hold a finger to my lips and fold my arms. She began telling what I hoped wasn't some long story. My legs have already been damaged enough from walking down endless stairs that could have been just one step and being run over more than once. I didn't need to get pins and needles as well as that. I mean, thank you very much, but I still want to be able to walk when I get older.

"The Scroll of Elysium is just like a normal human being, just like you or me. Well, maybe not me, seeing as I'm dead." She half grinned at me, and I felt a little tugging sensation on the top of my lip corners. Halleluiah! I'm stuck in the middle of time with my dead grandma who knows how to joke. I know it'd probably sound cool written down in a book somewhere, but, trust me, it's not all that it's cut out to be.

"Anyway, the Scroll of Elysium responds to people who know its background. It feels closer to it and to the person who has a grasp on the Scroll of Elysium's past and has bothered to find out about it. If it were to choose who it'd give his loyalty to between the most evil of all demons and the purest of angels, it would choose the demon if it knew more about it.

It responds the way a human would. It was made to have the feelings of a human. You see, when the Scroll of Elysium was made, the creator went to great lengths to capture a part of what controls the universe's happiness—hope. It lives on inside the Scroll, and this is what makes it so special. Without hope, love cannot possibly exist. I know that some people may differ in opinions, but it is true."

Aya paused to take in a breath, and I stared open-mouthed at her. She was a freaking genius. But there was one question that remained unanswered, and it was seriously bugging me. If there was anything that I couldn't stand more than my dysfunctional life, it was not knowing the answer to a question that somebody else knew the answer to. I felt as if I held in my question for more than a couple of seconds, my head would explode.

"Aya, who *was* the creator of the Scroll of Elysium?" I asked, holding my breath for some reason. This question felt oddly personal for some reason, but I don't see why it should be personal unless Aya had been the person who had created it. But that can't be possible. Can it? I knew the answer to my mental question even before Aya opened her mouth and closed her eyes that were now riddled with guilt for some reason, a reason that I was almost certain I knew the answer to.

"It was me, Beryl. I created the destruction of mankind. I am so sorry for causing this whole mess," Aya spoke softly, but it still sent a shock through me when she basically told me that she, my long lost granny, had been the person who created the worst weapon for her (once upon a time) own species.

I leaned back, stunned by what she had just told me. Aw, I wish "Show and tell" carried on throughout high school. I can guarantee mine would be the most interesting by far, only I wasn't exactly sure I was allowed to spill my guts to any random people at school.

"But why? Why would you create something that could mean the end of the world?" I blurted out, unable to shut my big mouth. I *had* to know why. I didn't know why, but there was a small part of me that desperately needed to know that the woman who had been my idol since I first heard of her wasn't some evil, old mastermind crook who wanted to destroy the world.

I felt oddly choked up, like I was about to start bawling, which is just not possible. Beryl Jones, ultimate freak of the century, never cries. Well, there are obviously some exceptions to that little rule of mine; but, oddly enough, it was true. It was like my tear ducts never formed while I was in my mum's stomach.

"Beryl, darling, you must understand why I did what I did. It seemed like a great idea at the time, and I was young, only sixteen—"

"My age . . ." I cut halfway through her sentence. She looked at me apologetically, but continued her story as if it was something she had been dying to get off her chest. *Dying* being metaphorically spoken, seeing as Aya was already dead in more than one way.

"I was sixteen years old. I had already lost everything that I could call family, and my powers had barely fully flourished." I opened my mouth as if I was going to say something (of course), but Aya gave me a look that all too clearly said that if I wanted to know why she'd made the Scroll of Elysium, I better shut my mouth and listen.

I closed my mouth pretty quickly, not wanting to get into her bad books. I mean, there *was* a reason why Aya had been the only person to survive the war.

"As I was saying, I was alone in a way. Sure, I had friends, but I had no one I could relive childhood memories with, no one who had seen me grow, and no one who was family or even from the same tribe as me. I was, what you would say now, depressed.

I cut off all of my new friends, anyone I knew who had contact with the outside world. I began to do the impossible. I stretched myself to unbelievable extents, forcing myself to achieve what nobody else had done.

I travelled back to my hometown, even though I knew that it was almost certainly overrun by the opposing tribe. It was empty though, devoid of all life. I sought out my former home and resurrected it in a way. I rebuilt it back to the way it was in the beginning when my family still walked on the earth. I didn't do it the magical way though. I built it the human way, the hard way.

In a way, every blister, sore, and millilitre of sweat was like a tribute to my dead family." Her voice sounded bitter, even now, so many years later.

"Once my past home had been rebuilt the way it looked like when I had been growing up, I came back to visit it for long periods of time. I would draw, paint, and sculpt ornaments while I was there. It was the only way to relieve myself from the pain of depression, but I knew I couldn't paint forever. It was one cursed day that I saw the piece of parchment that I had seen numerous amounts of times in my childhood. It seemed like fate to me. I thought, '*What if I could somehow find a way to make people like me happy?*'

And so, the idea of a Scroll of Elysium formed in my head. Little was I to know that it could be used as a weapon, as well as a medicine. Oh, if only my dear old mother had still been alive back then." She gave a dry chuckle but sobered up when the next horror washed through her mind. Pfft, knowing her, I didn't really want to know what she was thinking about now.

"The Scroll of Elysium was finally finished. It took almost all of my powers away. It got so bad that when I muttered the final enchantment, I passed out; all of my energy had been swept clean, away from my body and into the only living thing available—the Scroll of Elysium. That is the reason the Scroll of Elysium has human emotions.

Once I had reached my full health once again, I felt ambition burning through my body. I used the Scroll of Elysium in ways that helped me to escape depression. I was always full of hope, and I never gave up on any project that I started. I felt invincible. I was so happy that I didn't realise how the behaviour of my fellow villagers had altered.

There would always be a fight going on, and even the most loving couple would have a fight at least once every day. I was only aware of what I was feeling.

That all changed when I met Gregory." She gave an odd, girly giggle that made me want to puke. She reminded me *way* too much of Carla who was always giggling about one thing or another, mostly about her latest crush that seemed to change every three days—no joke.

"How did that help?" I asked, all agog for more juicy gossip but not really.

"I learnt how to love again," she said simply, as if this was the solution to all of the problems in the world. Well, thank you very much, but I'd rather have Einstein as my chemistry partner and not some lovey-dovey idiot who doesn't know what 1 + 1 is.

"I spread the happiness more equally and fairly, giving happiness and love to the people who needed it the most. Joy can be made every day, and it added to the happiness already in the Scroll of Elysium. For a while, life went on happily in my adopted village. We lived in matrimony until the town gossip that never seemed to like me followed me back to what was once my home.

Nobody knew where I was going every time I left the village except for Eloise. She was anxious to discover something about me that wasn't daisies and buttercups. Well, she didn't know that that was her lucky day. She saw me saying the enchantments used to provoke the power of the Scroll of Elysium. She immediately ran back to her village and started spreading rumours that I was some sort of witch and had some sort of magical instrument that contained hope. Little did she know that she was closer to the truth than any of the other villagers had thought.

Young children wouldn't go near me; adults would talk behind their hands about me and stop as soon as they saw me. If there was anything truer than the fact that grass is green, it's the fact that Eloise (the town busybody) never spoke anything but the truth.

I know this may seem a little odd for you, but the town gossips back then were not allowed to speak anything but the truth. There would be penalties for those who did other than that.

I began to fall into my little world of depression. I put a barrier between me and the outside world, which I didn't let anyone through. I only ever spoke to Lizzie; I didn't ever use the Scroll of Elysium. I felt in a way that it had betrayed me. Remember that the Scroll of Elysium has human qualities. I went to great lengths to try and destroy it. I burned it, tried to cut into pieces, threw it in a lake, but, every single time, I failed heavily.

Every morning, it would appear on my bedroom sill, looking fresh and brand new. Finally, I gave up on destroying it. By now, people were clamouring to see it. They may not have liked me, but they were still human; and, as humans go, they're always full to bursting point with curiosity." She gave me a pointed look that I (sensibly) chose to ignore. Excuse me, but as she had so kindly mentioned, I was still human, no matter how freaky I was.

She paused in her novel, remembering some long, faraway world that she would never get to see again. I looked at her, really looked at her as a young woman having to face the outside world all by herself with no family.

Jeez, if that was me, I would have killed myself long time ago. Either that or I would probably runaway screaming with a suitcase in my hands, full of books on witchcraft. Clearly, I did not get my courage from her.

"I did the only thing that could be expected. I hid it, far, far away where it was hidden from human reach. Unfortunately, I had to leave the village to do that, and it was certain that the villagers would assume that I was going off to destroy the world or something like that. Many people tried to stop me, but, thankfully, Lizzie, stood up for me in my defence; and, finally, I was given permission to leave the village without having to leave my home and find a new adopted tribe.

"It was one of the most stressful times of my life. People shunned me, I was feared by more and more people, and it didn't exactly help that I had red hair. It was a very widely known superstition that the demon colour was blood red, and, as you can so clearly see, my hair is almost exactly the same shade of red as that." She absently tugged a lock of her hair, and a dreamy look came over her face as she daydreamed about the old superstitions.

I only know one, and if I remember correctly, it has something to do with sweaty socks and body parts. Oh, thank god I was born in the twentieth century (Don't worry; I'm not 100 or something. I'm still young and sweet, even though my mother may disagree with me on the last part.)!

"When I had finally gotten permission to leave the village, I left as soon as I could. I hadn't told anybody why I had had to go so urgently all of a sudden, and I knew that that could very well have been the last time I saw any of my friends, but I knew I had to leave.

I travelled far across the country, taking to sea when I reached the country side. I didn't have a clear destination in mind, I just wanted to get as far as I could, away from what was once my home. I travelled all the way to what is now called Alaska.

There was a very large mountain there called *Haisfilg*, which means *might* in the ancient language. The people of the heavens now call it Mount Trievia. The tip of it emerges into the heavens; that is how large it is. It stands on a remote island that has not yet been discovered by mankind. I had been there once as a child with my family on a . . . holiday.

My grandmother had died, and she had always made it clear that if she were ever to die, she would want to be buried on a mountain where she would be close to where her power's roots lie. She could manipulate Earth." Oddly enough, this sounded perfectly normal to hear as if she was telling me her grandma was an accountant. Oh well, from what I've heard, anything's possible now.

"I had been forbidden as a child to climb the mountain, but I felt a strange pull towards it. I began the steep climb. It was a long, treacherous climb. I didn't have any of the equipment needed to climb the mountain, but I still struggled on. Remember, I had the Scroll of Elysium, and, in it, hope was stored.

I found an abandoned cave halfway up. It almost seemed to sing my name. Indeed, the wind whistling around it could have been mistaken for songs.

It seemed like the perfect hideout. The ground was earth, and, therefore, very easy to dig into. I dug long and hard for the next couple of weeks, wanting to make sure that it was as deep as it could possibly be. I put the Scroll of Elysium in a wooden crate, and put powerful enchantment over it that could only be broken by the most gifted of sorcerers. I even left a part of my soul back at the cave to protect the entrance." She paused for breath, and I took that as an opportunity to gawp at her.

Wow. The person (or ghost) had climbed a mountain. Clearly, I didn't get my stamina from Aya. I can barely climb a small hill, let alone a mountain. It must have helped that she had hope in her bag, but if it were me, I don't think even hope would have been able to stop me from giving up after the first step.

It seemed my plan had worked. I went back to the village, and the villagers must have noticed the decrease in the happiness and love. They blamed it all on me. Even my beloved Gregory seemed even more distant from me than he used to be. Even though I had succeeded in hiding the Scroll of Elysium, it was almost like the world had suddenly gone from bright and colourful to black and white.

It became so bad that in desperation, I tried to summon the spirits of my long gone mother and father. They were still a symbol of hope for me so many years later. They had always seemed so sure of everything when I was a child. That was my downfall. Many things are possible in the gifted world, but never, under any circumstances, can the dead be raised unless they summon themselves. Even then, it takes great amounts of energy and skill. I longed to smell my mother's sweet, flowery scent and hear my father's gruff voice one more time.

When it didn't work the first time I tried, I became filled with a dreadful sense of loss that seemed to be gnawing on my insides. I tried again and again, barely noticing how weak I was becoming. By this time, I was nearly senseless with grief. I could barely mouth the words of the incantation, my body weak from the sudden loss of energy. I collapsed as I repeated the words for what seemed the hundredth time. My body couldn't take it anymore.

By this time, I was ready to die. My body was ready to die. But somehow, I hung on. When I came around, it was night. I managed to make it back to the village by walking for short distances then resting. god knows how I managed that. I was never the same again.

Time freezers like me are supposed to live for hundreds of years. That is what makes us so rare. But nobody's perfect. They can die if they lose a certain amount of energy and spirit. I had already given up a part of my spirit to guard the Scroll of Elysium, making me more prone to death. That was the reason for my death just a couple of decades later." I stared at Aya. How can anyone talk about their death so casually? Not me, that's for sure.

Aya looked kinda tired like she had tried to raise her parents again, even though they were both dead (no offence). I don't know if it was just my terrible eyesight, but she seemed more transparent than she had been a couple of minutes earlier.

Oh, wait a second. She's supposed to be dead right? And like she just said, it takes energy to be visible to the living, right? Great, just when I'm really getting into her story, she becomes tired. Why me? I don't even like books, but you can't deny, she can tell a story.

"I thought that the Scroll of Elysium would still be safe after I died. The part of my spirit guarding it still remained even though I was long gone. It would have continued to be safe if I hadn't put my personal life before the safety of the Scroll of Elysium. I was still quite a young spirit and wasn't accustomed to the spirit ways.

I met a young child on one of my visits to what was once my home. He was now living there, and he saw me when I was practicing making myself visible to humans.

He was the spitting image of my grandson, Alfie, but a ten-year-old version. I couldn't help but feel love for him. I never knew his name. He was rather eager to know more about my history, but that wasn't what I found odd about him.

It was his eyes. They weren't normal human eyes. They had a depth to them, as if there was some hidden knowledge in them. It was like seeing the eyes of your great grandpa in your son's eyes after giving birth to him. It was most uncanny. I merely brushed it aside though, not really looking into it the way I ought to—"

"Wait." I cut in, feeling that if I didn't ask Aya this, I would burst with questions flying out of my body like a bomb. "How come that even though you are dead, you can still talk to me the way you are doing now and to your grandson thing?" I asked, not pausing to think if this would be offensive to her. My brain isn't exactly hardwired to receive emotional signals, so, really, all I could do was cross my fingers and hope that she wouldn't burst into tears and vanish on the spot.

Thankfully, she simply half-smiled and readily answered my question. Thank god she is nothing like my mum. She would have beaten me till my skin came off.

"Remember that everything that I was seeing and doing was in spirit form, and I could not stay down on the Earth for very long without becoming weak. Spirits are supposed to stay in the afterlife, but I was not content to do so. If I hadn't been gifted, I would not have been able to go to the land of the living.

As it is, it took me a lot of practice to be visible and audible to the living. I can show myself to people, but only to those who I wish to see me. For instance, if I was in a crowded room and I wanted to only show myself to you, I would merely focus on you. Spirits are all around us, but you can only sense and focus on those who have magical blood."

I gaped at her, surprised to the very core of my being. Wow, this world sure can't get any weirder. It's good to know that though. Now I can scare Carla to death every night when I tell her bedtime story. And this time, my mother can't tell me off for lying. Life is sweet.

"Now, as I was saying, I told him far too many things, and I even spoke about the one thing that I had sworn not to talk about: The Scroll of Elysium. Before long, he knew as much about the Scroll of Elysium as I did. He began asking me where it was hidden, but I never gave him the answer.

I remember one night, when he asked me if I loved him, not the grandson I once had but him as a person. I asked him why, and he told me that he didn't understand why I didn't trust him. He looked so upset, and he reminded me so much of Jack, and, even though I knew it wasn't him, I wanted nothing more than to get rid of the sadness in his old eyes. I foolishly told him where it was and how to get it.

I felt a moment of happiness when I saw the sadness leave his eyes, but it was instantly replaced with dread. I saw a maniacal flash of joy in his eyes that was not human. It scared me, and I left soon after, giving the excuse that I didn't have enough energy left to stay any longer.

The next day, when I went to check on the Scroll of Elysium, I found that it was gone. I could sense that its presence was no longer there with me in the cave. Once I was certain that the Scroll of Elysium was stolen, I went straight back to the little bungalow where the mirror image of my grandson had lived.

It was abandoned. There was not a living soul in the house, and it looked as if no one had ever lived there, much less a young boy and his whole family.

That was when I knew that, somehow, the young boy who looked like my grandson had found the Scroll of Elysium and was using it badly. The very air seemed greyer, and, everywhere you looked, miserable people could be seen roaming the streets, and children would be in their homes instead of playing on the streets. All around the little village where I had once lived, there were posters advertising the army and little ballot boards where every person over the age of sixteen had to write their name down to be recruited for the army. War was brewing, and, before long, it had started. You already know about the War of Crivial, I am assuming?"

Aya looked at me questioningly, her eyebrows slightly raised. She looked as though she thought I didn't know what on earth she was talking about.

I didn't get half of what she had said before, but if there was one thing I knew about, it would be the War of Crivial. Thank god for that. I mean, I was already seen as a typical knuckleheaded teenager of the twenty-first century in her eyes, and I didn't need stupid to be added to that impressive list of insults unless I wanted to break the world record for the most cussed person alive, which I most certainly do not.

I nodded once, not attempting to mask my impatience at the fact that she had stopped telling me her story. Oh, if only there was such thing as a publishing company back then. It would have been a number one bestseller and no prizes for guessing who would be the mad stalker who bought all of her books—me!

"I could only visit Earth for a limited amount of time, and, every time I went down to the living world, it seemed to be getting worse and worse. It would be normal to see heaps of bodies lying around in the streets with smoke rising haphazardly from it.

Women would be seen crying on their door steps with telegrams in their hands as they read the news that a loved one had been killed in war. It didn't help that there wasn't much hope if there was any at that time.

People became more suicidal, and there were a lot more deaths than there had been before. I knew that I had to do something, even though I didn't know what it was I could do to save those poor souls from themselves.

I spent years searching for him but to no avail. I would have found him much quicker if I had remembered the bond that I had with the Scroll of Elysium. It could not be helped. I was the creator of the Scroll of Elysium. I was like the mother of it. It felt a tie to me, and do not forget that I had left a part of my soul to protect the Scroll.

What I had not planned to happen was for my soul to forge as one with the Scroll of Elysium. It had still been guarding the Scroll of Elysium when that intruder took it. By some unknown, complex piece of sorcery, the Scroll of Elysium and the part of my spirit bonded and became merged into one being. I could feel that a part of my soul had merged with another. I didn't know how I could use this to my advantage though, so it wasn't much help.

I tried meditating for the very first time after one of my many visits to the living. I couldn't do much to help, but I needed to know what was going on. All I could do was wait for some miracle to happen. One visit affected me particularly. I had seen a young girl sitting on a doorstep by herself, her eyes blank and dazed.

She didn't look as if she was in this world. She couldn't have been more than six years old, yet she had a weariness surrounding her like an aura. It was something similar to what you would expect to find around the body of a ninety-two-year-old. It sickens me to this very day how she sat so simply, her chin resting on her spindly knees as she watched the world revolve around her while she sat on the same spot for all eternity.

I spent the next week or so meditating. It wasn't the mockery that is now used today in the modern society. It was deep and meaningful. You had to concentrate solely upon your subconscious and blank every single thing out. It took me only a week to trace the part of my spirit with the Scroll of Elysium. That was how easily within reach the answer to all of my problems was.

I tracked down the Scroll of Elysium, using only my spirit to help me. I can tell you now that that was no easy feat." She chuckled wryly.

"You had to concentrate solely on piecing together your soul as one again. If you lose your focus for even a split second, you would have to start again.

Of course, it wasn't too hard for me, seeing as I was nearly out of my mind with desperation to stop all of the pain and panic that I had caused. Even though I was not the person in possession of the Scroll of Elysium, the blame of what had happened rested solely on my shoulders.

If I had not been so selfish and created the Scroll of Elysium, that whole mess would never have occurred unless, of course, someone had been just as selfish a person as I had been *and* had magical abilities." She paused *again*, like all of this talking was wearing her throat—old women these days or, should I say, old female *ghosts* these days.

"Once I had traced the part of my spirit that was still with the Scroll of Elysium after all these years, I got the greatest shock of my life or, should I say, greatest shock of my death." I let out a snigger at that one. This is some, weird ghost.

I thought dead people were supposed to be sensitive about their deaths, not something to laugh about in a pub with the rest of your ghost pals. Guess this isn't the first thing that I've been wrong about though, so it wasn't exactly surprising to be wrong about something else.

"I found him sitting in a rather large mansion. I believe if you were to see it, you would call it 'huge' or 'humungous,' whatever those ghastly words mean. It had hundreds of windows lined up in neat rows and had to be at least seven storeys high. What I saw when I went inside was rather different to what I had had in mind.

I had been expecting to see a little imitation of my grandson sitting on the floor of a grand nursery, not a fully grown man sitting inside an office. It was a most shocking sight. If you had the power of being able to read minds, I would show it to you in perfect clarity, but, alas, you cannot—"

"I can!" I exclaimed, my voice stronger than I could have hoped for. I may not be a boaster, but thank you very much; I wasn't about to sit by and miss out on what could be an opportunity of a lifetime. I could be about to delve into the memories of a ghost that lived before the dinosaurs. Excuse me for wanting to do it.

Aya looked steadily into my eyes. She didn't say anything. She looked at me for so long that I slowly felt my mental barriers crumble to ashes. I tried to look away and give her some privacy, but I couldn't look away from her eyes that I suddenly seemed to be drowning in.

Uh-oh, it was happening again. I was sinking into her memories. The scenery around me was fast changing, blurring into one another as they morphed into what Aya had once seen and was now reliving . . .

CHAPTER 10

Bang! I fell down heavily onto what felt like a solid wooden floor. I would probably have broken my neck if I hadn't landed on a thick rug in front of a heavily decorated wooden desk. Thank god for that, even though it wasn't exactly comfortable.

Ever since I found out who and what I was, I've been saying god more and more, to the point where you would think that I was some sort of female vicar. Funny, I never thought I would turn out to be religious.

I sat up, massaging my head that had seemed to land on the ground before the rest of my body had reacted to gravity. Why me? It seems like luck is avoiding me more than usual. I mean, I may not have brittle bones that snap at any sudden movement, but I'm certainly not one of the competitors in the Olympics. If I was, I sure wouldn't be here.

I got up wincing with my hands still on my head. Standing may have been more tiring, but if I sat on the ground for another minute, my spine would be permanently damaged, and I'd live out my days in a wheelchair. That's only if I didn't die of a heart attack before I reached the wheelchair stage.

I glanced around the room, drinking every aspect of it. It was so old-fashioned that I wanted to laugh out loud. Even the man sitting behind the desk and writing some sort of letter looked kinda old. Wait . . . man? There was a man in the same room as me? Oh crap!

I slowly turned my body around so that I was facing the desk. Call me stupid, but I wasn't about to let the man sitting in the chair shoot me in the back before I could explain myself. I looked at the man who was still writing his letter peacefully. He didn't look older than thirty, but the little strands of gray hair on his head gave him away.

He had broad shoulders and pitch black hair that flowed down his back. He had huge hands that would look better on a gorilla and long hairy arms that looked as if they could knock a world-class boxer out. Jeez, if I was married to him, the first thing I would do is book him to a waxing salon.

I cleared my throat as loud as I could and waited for a sign that the man sitting in front of me wasn't some robot that wrote letters for a living. Sadly, my suspicions were confirmed. He continued writing as if he was the only person that lived on this planet.

"I see you have now got some things to sort out with the international rulers." A crisp voice that could shatter glass broke the silence that was getting unbearably awkward, even though I was the only person who was aware of that. I yelped and my hand flew over my mouth as if to stifle my screams.

I whirled around, my eyes darting into every little corner to try and see who it was that had spoken. There was no one to be seen.

The man sitting at the desk still didn't move an inch. That's it. This person sitting in front of me could not be human.

"Show yourself, beloved." The man finally raised his head and spoke. This nearly shocked me into a heart attack. I was beginning to think he was mute! But, then again, I was in a memory, so I should be more concerned if the man spoke to me.

"Do not call me by that name," the voice spat into the silence. The tension in the room was so high that I felt like getting a power saw out and drilling it through the air. The only thing on my mind was cutting the tension, and there seemed no other way to do it than getting out a power saw and slashing wildly at the air. Or I could just make life easier for myself and the people who work at asylums and just kill these people, although I'm pretty sure you can't die more than once. Plus the people in the medieval prisons would have to deal with me so I wouldn't be helping anyone.

I settled for trying to locate the voice that sounded more like the voice of a cranky headmaster than of a ghost in an old man's house. No offence to all of the old people who think they're still twenty-one years old.

The echo of the voice was still bouncing around the room like a tennis ball that was being hit between Andy Murray and Roger Federer. I shivered involuntarily.

Why on earth was the man smiling like Christmas had come early? I, at least, had some idea about who was speaking, but I wasn't exactly jumping around singing nursery rhymes was I? And yet, this huge ball of bone and flesh was sitting there in his chair smiling like the buffoon he was.

"Show yourself," he repeated, but this time he sounded businesslike and not like a doting wife who was greeting her husband after a long day at work.

When Aya (wild guess) still didn't show herself, his look of delight changed into one of contempt. "Huh. I never cut you out for a coward Ayasia. Guess dying brought something different out in you."

Ayasia. Hmm, so that was her full name. I was beginning to think that Aya's parents were sailors who couldn't stop saying, "Ahoy there!"

Calling Aya a coward had struck a nerve though. I could almost feel her debating her choices: not show herself and come off as a coward or show herself and look like a dead person with no backbone (metaphorically speaking). I could almost hear her thoughts clicking together. There was a faint shimmer in the air directly in front of the door, and, slowly, Aya came into view.

A flash of triumph sparked in the man's eyes, but was quickly diminished as Aya's hawklike stare focused on him. I had to give it to him. He was a damn good actor.

She looked exactly the same with her waterfall of red velvet cascading down her back and eyes that could burn through metal literally. How the man managed to stay alive with her gaze trained on him, I have no idea.

"Where is the boy?" It was more a demand than a question. The man's smile became even more pronounced.

"I am not here to fool around. *Where is the boy?*" She sounded like butter wouldn't melt in her mouth. Seeing as she was dead, it probably wouldn't, but you get the picture. She wasn't here to mess around.

"Oh, but I am not joking Ayasia. Have you not realised it yet?"

"I do not have the time for riddles or jokes. I only came here to get the boy. I know that he is here, and the Scroll of Elysium is somewhere near here too. Now, tell me where he is, and I shall consider letting you see the daylight of tomorrow." Aya's voice had turned menacing and her eyes were getting narrower and narrower.

This was something that I was forced to see on my mother's face every single morning when she found our pet gerbil in the pantry eating the bread and muffins. In other words, this was a sign that Aya was going to blow soon, and anyone standing closer than five metres away from her was going to get seriously hurt.

"If you're sure." With a dark laugh, the man stood up from his seat and threw his arms open wide. He began muttering an assortment of the strangest sounding words that would look more at home coming out from a baby's mouth. They sounded oddly familiar though, as if I had heard these words said before.

You know that feeling you get when you hear a something in your language that you haven't heard before, but you know that it is from your language? Yeah, that's exactly how I felt. What gets me is that the only language I know is English, and I suck at modern languages.

Oh well. Maybe knowing languages from around the world come as a package deal with having psychic abilities and mind reading. Can't say I'd object to that. I'd have a guaranteed A+ in modern languages.

I focused on the man, sensing that something wasn't quite right with him. He seemed kind of blurry on the edges, almost like he was having an extra fast spastic attack. He looked as though he was melting in a human microwave, and his chants got louder and faster than before.

From out of nowhere, there came a loud *thwump* sound, and there was a bright light that nearly made my abused eyes go blind. I shut my eyes, watching as the light turned my eyelids red and as it slowly faded to a cool black again; I opened my eyes. What I saw shocked me to the core of my existence. In the place where the man had been standing now stood a young boy around ten years old with floppy brown hair in his eyes. It was Aya's grandson.

Aya stared for what seemed to be an age before she shook her head and closed her eyes as if to shake the image away from her eyes. If it wasn't for the suit that was draped over his body 100 sizes too big, he could have been a photograph of the young boy I had seen before.

"No," Aya muttered, her voice breaking slightly with her eyes still squeezed shut.

"Oh yes, Ayasia. Have you not figured it out yet? I have always known that you were dim-sighted, but it seems even my expectations were too high for you. Even a fool could have figured it out by now. How could a mere ten-year-old boy find the Scroll of Elysium and use it to make the world a better place like the way I have done? It would have been impossible. Only I could have accomplished something like this." He taunted her, his now young eyes flashing with no mercy.

He looked like that Chinese boy from the *Karate Kid* that was beating the crap out of Dru. Surprisingly, I felt pity surge up through me for Aya, even though I knew it was ridiculous to feel this way. I mean, come on, this happened like a million years ago, and yet here I was about to burst into tears while watching the memory of some old (no offense) hag.

"Nathanial," Aya uttered his name with enough venom in it to fill a thousand or so death adders. Beware, all mice around the world. The man/boy smiled evilly, his soft, cherubic face not matching the twisted expression on it. It was like combining a Chihuahua with a bulldog.

"Oh yes, Ayasia. You have finally solved the 'equation.' How could you ever think that I would leave you once your whole family was dead? That would not have been enough Ayasia; oh no, it wouldn't have been. You know why I destroyed your village. You know why I came for you. If only you had not been so stubborn and unwilling, then I may have spared your village. It is your fault Ayasia that your family is now rotting deep within the Earth or wherever it is you bury your dead." Nathanial chuckled menacingly, and it was quite shocking to see the boy's face contort with maliciousness and transform into the face of a young bully.

"Why? Why would you do this? You told me once that you loved me, and you end up killing my whole family, the same family that took you in when you most needed help. Why?" Whoa. Back up. Since when did the baddie fall in love with the hero? This is some seriously messed-up fairytale.

Aya's voice remained calm and steady, but you could tell that he had gotten to her. Maybe it was mentioning her family that had gotten this reaction from her.

"Oh, Ayasia, I never loved you. That same fool could have figured that out. I needed to know how powerful your . . . kin were. And by god, they were powerful. I had to . . . recruit about a dozen villagers to get powers sufficient enough to even destroy one person. You do know that is a compliment, don't you?"

Aya's look of pure hatred silenced him but only for a couple of seconds. "Well, I was young and foolish back then. And there were only two things on my mind—finding power, and getting power.

When I first found out about your tribe, I thought you would be an ideal start to a powerful tribe that none could defeat. You had it all: power, grace, and even looks. You were ideal. Unfortunately, your tribe wasn't exactly cooperative. You see . . ."

"I know all of this already. Why on earth would I want to hear my life's history repeated from the lips of the man who has done absolutely nothing other than wreck my life again and again? You would think destroying my living life would be enough, but, no, you have to completely and utterly demolish my afterlife as well. I came here for one thing and one thing only. Give me the Scroll of Elysium, and I shall put our whole encounter right at the very back of my mind where it belongs." Aya's eyes were glinting with vindictive fury, and the tips of her ears were slowly turning redder and redder.

Jesus, this whole replaying of events from the past was seriously giving me a bad headache. It was like watching HD TV through cling film, although I'm pretty sure that Aya looked a lot more wispy and delicate now than she did when I first saw her. Crap (mind my language)! She was losing more and more energy every minute, and if my calculations were correct (unlikely), she would completely vanish in about five minutes.

Why? Excuse me, but I really want to finish this before she flies away or whatever it is that spirits do these days. The way things are going, they've probably got their own private jets and helicopters.

"Oh, I am sure that you would love to hear your history from the point of view of the man you hate and brought your whole life crashing down within minutes." Oh, he knew how to make a person agitated, much less a woman. If it was my mother he was speaking to, he'd have a knife at his throat and a gun at his head by now.

You could tell that despite everything that had happened, Aya was still curious to know what happened. Nathanial took Aya's silence as his cue to carry on talking.

"As I was saying, your tribe seemed ideal for the job. My aim in life was quite simple—get power; use the power. And your village seemed the quickest way to fulfil my life's need.

Your tribe was not cooperating, but I could not give up. I knew that even if I was to make a powerful tribe that was undefeatable, you and your kin would set about demolishing it. So I did the next best thing to enslaving you all—I tried to bring you down. And

I thought I did until your beloved child somehow managed to communicate with my own.

"Archie and Andrea have never tried to communicate with you. They don't even know who you are for crying out loud. They couldn't have tried to speak with you."

"Oh, but they did. You mustn't have been giving them the attention that they so badly needed, especially Andrea."

"Andrea . . ." Aya took in a breath that nearly knocked her of her feet. She completely vanished for a second but reappeared with a look of distinct shock plastered onto her face. I nearly choked on my saliva. She looked as if she was on a rollercoaster, and her seat had gone flying off the ride.

"Yes, Andrea. It seems as if you weren't giving her the love that she needed. Oh, you didn't give them any at all. You weren't even at home. It's no wonder they turned out the way they did. You were off helping me destroy the world even if you didn't know it at the time—"

"Don't you dare say another word about my children, or it'll be the last thing you say," Aya said in a smooth icy voice that sent shivers down my back. Whoa. This crazy old woman meant business. "Oh, whatever you say, dearest one," he said silkily, not looking in the least ruffled. "As I was saying, you didn't give her love. Oh, I am sure you loved her, but you didn't exactly show it to them, did you ?"

Aya gave him a dirty look but kept silent. "Well, Andrea didn't appreciate you shrugging her of like a piece of dirt. So she came to me, your one and only sworn enemy. I fused a part of her spirit with mine without her knowing, but her body couldn't handle the magnificence of my soul. So she died. A part of my spirit remained with her, and, once she had been dead for four cycles of the moon, when her spirit had completely left her body and her soul was joined as one in the after world, I had a chance to have an insight into your life. It seemed perfect. It was almost as if it was meant to be. I had the perfect opportunity to watch you.

I wanted you dead, Ayasia, even if you were not aware of it then. And I knew I would succeed. I just never thought that you would be the one to create your own destruction and my glory.

I knew that something was wrong. I knew that you were leaving the village for prolonged amounts of time. And I must admit that I was rather curious as to what you were doing. So I followed you on one of your vacations. Well, not me but the part of my spirit that had been severed from the rest of my soul. And my, my, my, what I saw gave me quite a shock." Aya bowed her head down as though she knew what he was going to say, and she was ashamed of it.

"The Scroll of Elysium," Aya half-whispered softly. Her whole body slumped inwards like she couldn't hold up her nonexistent body any longer.

"Yes, Ayasia. I watched you make the key to my success. And I am sure that you have figured out the rest of my little fairytale."

"But how? You couldn't have found the Scroll of Elysium without me telling you, and I never told a single soul."

"Except for one little boy, a boy who goes by the name of Alfie and calls you his grandmother, a boy who you would trust your life with, even though he was so young, a boy who you once loved."

Aya's face had been growing more desperate and wild since she the minute she stepped into Nathanial's "office," but, now, she looked more animal than human or whatever it is that she is.

"That boy was not Alfie. He couldn't have been. Alfie died a long time ago—" Aya's eyes sharpened as she regarded Nathanial whose eyes had gone alight with glee like a little kid.

God, childish or something? And this man claims to be older than Christ himself. I'd hate to know what he was like when he was my age. "It was you, wasn't it? You're a Chineydu, aren't you?" Chineydu? Isn't that the name of spirits who've died and come back using the body of another corpse? Thank god I listen during history class.

"Yes, Ayasia, I am a Chineydu. I thought you of all people would have realised that by now."

Aya opened her mouth to say something, but, suddenly, I could hear no more. I could see her mouth moving, but I could hear no words. The room was changing swiftly back into Pelesmia, and I closed my eyes, waiting for it to morph back into reality.

*   *   *

My eyes opened of its own accord. I could see Aya sitting across from me, watching me cautiously like she thought I would bolt the minute she turned her head. I stared at Aya with my mouth in my lap. Now is the time for Botox on my mouth and cheeks. What's wrong with me? I just saw a memory that would have gotten me into rehab if I even told anyone about it; and yet I was thinking about Botox? I blame my mother entirely.

"Was . . . was that all real?" I asked—great. What a stupid thing to ask. I may as well have asked her if elephants were bigger than spiders. Aya gave a quick sharp nod. I kept my expression neutral and waited for Aya to say something. At last, she opened her mouth.

"You should go now," Aya said. What? That was *not* what I was hoping to hear from her. I was thinking more of an "I'll tell you why the hell I showed you all of that."

"But how am I going to get back—" Before I could finish my sentence, the whole world seemed to turn upside down (literally), and Aya slowly faded away.

"Use what is said to your advantage . . . ." A voice whispered, its voice trailing delicately to me on the gentle wind. But I still needed to ask her something before she left me.

"Aya! Was that Nathanial you were telling me about the same one who tried to kill Adira?"

"Trust in yourself, young one . . ." Aya said before she completely disappeared. What type of an answer was that? I thought she was supposed to help me, not give me more riddles to figure out. Thank you very much, but I've got enough in my head right now. What happened to giving teenagers some slack?

I closed my eyes, waiting for the room to stop spinning round and round. When I finally felt the place judder to a halt, I was greeted by the most ferocious pain in my head, and it wasn't pleasant. I managed to open my eyes for a second, and all I could hear were screaming women and the sound of footsteps running. Adira looked as if she was about to faint, and, before I could do anything else, the pain in my head became too much for me, and I gave in to the blackness that was pulling me. I hope it's not death.

CHAPTER 11

"Beryl! Wake up child! Yeesh! This child won't even wake up for her own mother. See how these children of mine disrespect me so?" That voice sounded oddly familiar, not in a good way at all. In fact, it sounded a lot like my mother. But god wouldn't be so mean as to bring my mother all the way from wherever she was and dump her on to me. Still, just to be sure, I opened one of my eyes and gave a little yelp when I saw my mother's face directly above mine and so close to me that it looked like she had only one eye in the middle of her forehead.

"Now you wake up! I've been going out of my mind in the last couple of days! How do you think I felt when I got a phone call saying that you were hit by a chariot and that I had to come straight to Morpheus!" My mother blared on, seemingly unaware of the pain she was causing me and not just physically but emotionally as well.

Since when did mother know anything about Morpheus and chariots? I barely knew anything about them either, and I was the one with the magic powers. My mother showed no sign of slowing down in her lecture, so I took it as an opportunity to look around the room and at my surroundings.

Every single thing was gold. It was like someone had been let loose in the hospital with only gold spray paint to give them company. Even the nurse's skin was gold. I glanced down at myself to see that I was also wearing a gold tunic. Sheesus Christ, these people sure have obsessive compulsory problems.

"Where . . . where am I?" I asked wearily, bracing myself for the answer. The side of my face stung as I stretched a long cut. The room was way too familiar for my liking. I was almost certain that I had been here, even though that was absolutely ridiculous. I've only been to a hospital once, and that was because I broke my arm, not because I had been run over by a chariot. It was like a bad case of déjà vu.

"You're in Morpheus, hospital for the magically gifted." A nurse popped out of nowhere like a magician's act. Seriously, how hard did I hit my head? I could've sworn she wasn't there a second ago.

I looked around the room long and hard, determined to understand why it seemed as if I'd been in this room before without being run over. But to do that in peace, I had to subject myself to humiliation and give mother an opportunity to rant at me.

"Why am I here? I'm supposed to be in bed with Chuchu right now," I said, grimacing slightly at my mother's look of shock. I mean, Chuchu fell out of the boot of our car when we were going to a beach in Bournemouth. Oh well, at least it worked. Mum started ranting like a mad woman.

This time, I didn't pay any attention to her. I looked around the room, trying to figure out why the room looked so familiar! If only I was psychic I'd be able to figure it out. Wait . . . I am psychic. Wow.

I am the world's biggest dufus. This must have been the vision that I had earlier on! I really am an idiot. Even a four-year-old would have been able to figure that out.

Instead of trying to get up and having to experience that horrible pain all over again, I simply lay on the bed and stared up at the ceiling waiting for mother to finish her lecture.

"Well? Did you?" My mother was eyeing me like she thought I wasn't listening. Pfft, like I was. I quickly looked her in the eye and found that she wanted to know if I'd done my geometry. Gee, Ma, why don't you ask me how I'm feeling? No wonder Dad died. He was probably imagining her being sweet, and he had a heart attack. "Yeah, Ma."

Before she could give me another lecture, the nurse spoke up. "Ma'am, I am terribly sorry, but I am afraid you will have to leave now." God help this poor woman. Mother looked as if she was about to let rip. I was almost about to yell a warning to the nurse, but something in my mother changed. She visibly relaxed, and her eyes went all dreamy.

"Yes madam. I think I would like a drink." She walked out of the room unsteadily, following yet another gold-cladded nurse. Adira walked in a second later, looking slightly surprised when mother walked straight into the wall and shook her head tipsily like she had just drunk a whole barrel full of vodka.

I looked at her cautiously, unsure of what to say. I mean, she had just told me her life story practically, and it can't have been too easy to tell someone that you want to kill on a daily basis, that you lived in an orphanage as a child, and that you were almost killed by someone you trusted.

She came and sat in the chair next to me just like the first time I met her, only before, I had been hit by a car; and, this time, it was a chariot. Oh well, the older you get, the more fancy your accidents are.

"Adira! What the hell happened? How is mother here? Please don't tell me she's magically gifted as well! That's the last thing I need right now." The last thought nearly gave me a heart attack. Mother? Doing magic? Excuse me for being a snob to my own mother, but those two phrases do not go together at all. Oh, god. It was the only explanation though. How else could she be here without being a mad stalker? Oh god, please don't answer that.

"Beryl, seriously, how hard did you hit your head? Your mother is no closer to being magically gifted than Michael Jackson is." Thanks a lot Adira for comparing my mother to a person who doesn't have a permanent nose of all things. No offence Mr. Jackson, wherever you are.

"We gave your mum Ambrosia. It has a different effect on mortals than it would have on a magically gifted person." My look of alarm must have alerted Adira that I wasn't completely happy with her answer. "She's not going to die or anything. She'll simply forget everything that has happened today."

"What was the point of letting her see me if she's just going to forget?"

"Er, we thought that it would be more comforting for you to know that someone you knew was with you." Pfft, she'd clearly never met my mother before if she thought she would come to comfort me. It's more likely that she'd pole dance in the middle of St. Paul's cathedral.

"What happened though?" I mean, it was kind of obvious that I had been hit by a vehicle of some sort, but it'd help if I got a firsthand account of what happened.

"Well, you already know that you were hit by a chariot. That was normal enough; we could have cured you instantly but something seemed to happen after you were hit. You kind of had a . . . fit. You started shaking around uncontrollably, and there was nothing we could do. We brought you here to Morpheus. As far as I know, you didn't wake up until just now, which means you've been unconscious for about 3 hours."

Wow. I must have been more tired than I thought I'd been. Either that or I was suffering from a bad case of jetlag, even though it took a second for me to get to Pelesmia.

"So?" Adira's voice cut though my thoughts.

"So what?" Adira gave me a filthy look though I was annoying her on purpose. As if. I didn't even know what on earth she was talking about.

"What happened when you were supposedly knocked out for 3 hours?" Duh, sometimes, I seriously think I'm amnesic. I forget things too easily to be completely normal. I opened my mouth and talked, and talked, and talked, and talked, and talked for about fifteen minutes nonstop about what had just happened to me.

Surprisingly, Adira didn't ask me questions every two seconds. She probably asked me every five seconds. My voice got hoarser and hoarser the longer I spoke, and I'm guessing that doctors wouldn't recommend speaking for this long unless I wanted tonsillitis.

After I finished talking, I leaned back and looked at Adira. She looked as if she already knew everything that I just told her. Pfft, I thought I was supposed to be the psychic.

After a long minute, Adira spoke. "Beryl. We have to go to Mount Trievia as soon as possible." Superman to the rescue! No prizes for guessing who Lois Lane was and who was holding him back—moi. But I honestly think something happened to Adira while I was knocked out. Maybe she was so heartbroken that I had nearly died that she tried to commit suicide by hitting her head with a hammer.

As unlikely as that may seem, I could imagine it all too clearly. Stop! Why on earth am I thinking about Adira killing herself when the world could end at any second? Okay. Focus.

"Adira, how are we supposed to find this mountain? I mean, if Pelesmia is as large as you say it is, then how on earth are we supposed to find a mountain, let alone a mountain tip?" I was at least trying to be reasonable. Plus I didn't much fancy trekking around the whole of the heavens without having a clue as to what was going on.

"Beryl, I wouldn't expect you to try and find a mountain peak, which is why I'm not even going to try and find it . . ."—thank god—" because I already know where it is." Dang! I thought I was getting off lightly for once in my life! Guess not.

"The mountain Trievia is hidden away from the people of Pelesmia. It is forbidden to enter there." Great, we weren't only going to climb a mountain, but we were going to climb a forbidden mountain that none had climbed before. This was so not turning out to be my type of day.

"But how do we know that the Scroll of Elysium is even there?" I asked. Hadn't Aya taken it away from Nathanial and hid it again? It could be in the middle of the Pacific for all we know.

"You told me that Aya told you that the Scroll of Elysium was like a human." I nodded, uncertain. "Well, humans do not like to get uprooted. They would prefer to stay in the place where they have lived. Say a person called Jill had to move to Australia from England. There would always be the chance that Jill wouldn't like her new environment.

And if the Scroll of Elysium doesn't like its environment, there's always the chance that it wouldn't function properly. And Aya can't take a risk like that. It would endanger mankind's survival. It was risky enough moving the Scroll of Elysium to Mount Trievia, but she had to. Thankfully, the Scroll of Elysium was content with its surroundings." Ok. I could understand that. But still.

"How can you be sure?" I asked. I really wasn't trying to be a pain in the neck, but I could see that I was really annoying her.

"Because of this." She reached into the satchel she had slung around her shoulders and took out Aya's diary. Funny, I never thought that Adira was a thief. Adira flicked to a page near the end of Aya's journal and shoved it into my lap without even asking me if my legs were still hurting from my little accident (i.e. getting run over by a chariot). Clearly, Adira was suffering from some little health problems—mentally.

"Look here." Adira pointed to the little piece of text bang in the middle of the page. Pfft, like I could read that. The writing was so small that you would need three magnifying glasses layered up on top of each other to make sense of even one word.

I gave Adira *"The Look."* She rolled her eyes and gave a posh little huff like she thought she was the queen of England. She picked the book up from her lap and brought it up close to her face.

"The Scroll of Elysium has a unique way of understanding its surroundings. If the place it is accommodating is not up to its standards, it will go into hibernation, taking away most of the world's happiness. This is fatal, and severe bouts of depression will befall the world and the people living in it. It has happened before, and there are severe consequences. The depression will only end once the Scroll of Elysium is ready to come out of hibernation. The time or place cannot be chosen or determined. It can stay in hibernation for centuries if it wants to. The slightest change in its accommodations can cause a great tragedy." Adira looked up at me with smugness etched into every feature. Even her ears seemed to radiate victory. For once, I had no argument to defend myself with.

"Okay, the Scroll of Elysium is probably still in Mount Trievia; but how on earth are we going to get there in the first place? It's not like they're going to let me walk out of the hospital after I got run over." At least, that's what I think. That's what happens on planet Earth most of the time unless the doctor is treating his ex-wife or something like that.

"Leave that to me." Adira got this look in her eyes that frightened me. Well, frankly, she scares me full stop. She got up from her chair, grabbed her satchel, and practically flew out of the room. I stared at her open-mouthed, my eyes round with AS pennies.

I looked at her chair, which she had been sitting on not so long ago, and saw Aya's diary lying open on the edge of the chair. I sighed and leaned across the edge of the bed to pick it up. Oh well, at least she had left something to keep me company in what I thought was going to be a long wait. Every cloud has a silver lining. Just keep telling yourself that, Beryl.

*   *   *

I seriously cannot believe Adira. She had no sympathy whatsoever for me, even though I had just nearly been killed. We were in a chariot, on our way to what would probably be our deaths. Adira had done her freaky mind control thing on the doctors and nurses there, and they let me leave the hospital without a backwards glance.

I honestly think Adira was taking this thing way too far. Yeah, I know the whole world's fate rested on the choices that we would soon be making, but still. I had just been run over. And I don't think the whole jug of ambrosia that Adira had forced down my throat was going to help me much. I felt half-dead.

We were on some kind of chariot drawn by two horses. It was similar to what Shrek and Fiona had driven in on their way to Far, Far Away. In this case, Adira was Donkey, annoying me to death.

It was getting foggier and foggier the more we rode out of Pelesmia. We were now out of the "posh" part of Pelesmia, and were now reaching the slums. We drove past people who looked like they hadn't eaten a decent meal in years, sitting calmly on the ground.

They didn't look upset or hungry though. Each person was sitting with their legs crossed underneath a tree with their eyes closed. They didn't look as though they were breathing. It was deathly quiet, and the horse's hooves thumping the barren ground sounded like meteors falling onto earth.

"The astrologers of Pelesmia," Adira whispered to me. She was sitting on the uncomfortable bench . . . next to me. She was staring out of the chariot looking awestruck. Now that we were closer to the astrologers, I could see that every single one of the people was a man, and there wasn't a single child, much like there wasn't any sound.

"They meditate all day, trying to reach inner peace. They are all humans who have managed to make it to the heavens through meditation and starvation."

"Like you," I whispered back. I wasn't trying to annoy her; I just wasn't really thinking right. The astrologers made me feel really safe, like I could say whatever I wanted and face no consequences. They looked so peaceful and calm that I half-felt like jumping out from the carriage and meditating alongside them.

"If I had wanted, I could have continued to meditate once I had reached Pelesmia, but I knew that astrology wasn't the path for me. I didn't even believe in star signs back when I was a human," Adira whispered back.

I was going to ask her how exactly she thought she was going to become an astrologer when they were clearly all men, but I thought better of it. It felt really weird to even whisper in the hushed silence of the place. You could tell that before we had come bumbling into the astrologers home, not one sound had even been breathed for a

197

long, long time. How they managed to cough and sneeze without making any noise is something I do not understand.

We were soon out of the astrologer's meadow and were driving over an abandoned stretch of land. The road we were driving on suddenly disappeared and we were now bumping along bare earth. I can tell you now, from experience, that it wasn't exactly comfortable to be thrown around a cramped carriage. There were rocks and pebbles scattered randomly across the dry sand, and even the slightest gust of wind would send them tumbling around all over the place.

At least twenty pieces of grit had to have landed in my eyes. It stung like crazy. I've always thought that mother was exaggerating when she told me that I wasn't allowed to go to the beach because the sand might get into my eyes and blind me permanently. Right now, I was on the verge of actually believing her. I know! Shocking, isn't it? Maybe the astrologer's meadow had messed up my brain somehow.

I leaned my head against the carriage, closed my swollen-feeling eyes, and rested my hand against it, trying to cool them down. It would have helped if I had a wet cloth with me, but by the looks of it, we were in the middle of a desert, and the only water I was going to see was if I was having hallucinations.

I yawned and gazed out into the never-ending desert. Getting run over had really messed up my sense of time. It felt as though it was midnight, not one o'clock in the afternoon. I really needed to catch up on my sleep if I was planning on waking up tomorrow. Surely, one quick little nap wouldn't do any harm . . .

*   *   *

I awoke to the sound of the taxi driver speaking some next up language that sounded vaguely like English and gesturing wildly at Adira. Adira was giving him puppy dog eyes and appeared to be begging him for something.

Why she didn't just possess his mind and make him do whatever it was that she wanted him to do, I have no idea. Maybe it was because of the man's Hitler moustache. People with Hitler moustaches tend to be more evil than other people. If my mother was a man, she'd have ten heads, and every single head would have a Hitler moustache.

"No. No can do. I drive you too close to ze mountains, and dat is dat. I will not drive one more millimetre. Zat iz it. You leave now please, or come home wid me." It was bad enough trying to understand his thick accent, but it was even worse when I figured out what he was saying. He was basically saying, get out of my chariot, and we will each go our own ways; or come with me, and pay me my money, and I will take you back to where you were in the first place—harsh, right?

"Are you absolutely sure that you cannot drive any further up?"

"Yes, I am very, very, verrry sure indeed. Do not ask me again, or I vill be very, very, verrry angry." Damn, this man meant some serious business. It was actually kind of funny. This puny little man who barely reached my shoulders was threatening to dump us in the middle of nowhere. But you could tell that he was deadly serious. His small chinky eyes oozed sincerity behind his outsized specs.

"Okay. I understand sir. I am sorry to have disturbed you like this." Without another word, Adira handed the chariot driver a small handful of coins and walked away. It was only when the chariot driver climbed back into the carriage that I realised that Adira was outside, and I was still inside with a psycho man who was going to drive off to Timbuktu in a couple of seconds.

"You are going, or you are staying lady?" the man asked me.

"Um, I'm going. Sorry." I climbed out, and stood outside blinking for a couple of seconds. It took me a minute to process what I was seeing. It was a completely desolate wasteland that yelled: "Go back to where you came from, or you will suffer!—painfully!"

There were old abandoned cottages thrown here and there randomly, and there was not a single person around. Everything looked grey, like someone had sucked all the life and energy out of this place. Even the air seemed gray. Overall, this place was not exactly a place where you would want to raise your kids.

Adira was at least five metres away, and it was pretty clear that she was not going to wait for me to catch up with her. Either that or she thought I was Usain Bolt or something, which I most certainly am not. I can barely do track at school.

"So what's the game plan?" I asked when I finally caught up to Adira. She gave me a dirty look as if I had insulted her mother. Well, that'd be pretty hard to do, seeing as her mumma was six feet under for about seven centuries now.

"There is no game plan. You are merely here to help me find the Scroll of Elysium. All you have to think about is getting the Scroll of Elysium without dying. The rest is my concern." Jeez. Well, someone clearly got out of the wrong side if the bed today if she even slept, which I very much doubted.

We carried on walking through the muck of whatever it was we were in. We had to have walked for at least ten more minutes before we came to a sort of maze entrance.

On top of the two hedges, there was an old, broken down sign that had something written there in a language that I had never seen. It looked like Amharic and French combined.

"Chilowa le soa fangh ah herallee prois as ophegif," Adira rattled off.

Well, if she thought I understood a word of what she had just said, she was completely off her rocker. "It's basically saying, 'Adventurers beware, if your intentions are evil, your deeds and thoughts shall be sought out.'" Wow. I've heard friendlier things coming out of my mother's mouth, and that was saying something.

"Well?"

"Well what?"

"Will we have to hack through the jungle to get to the mountain where the Scroll of Elysium is supposed to be hidden?"

"Looks like it. And something's telling me that this isn't going to be a normal maze." Adira sounded defeated, like she already knew that there was no chance in hell that we were going to be able to find the Scroll of Elysium.

"Well, we might as well try." Without another word, I squared my shoulders and took the first step into the jungle. Instantly, I could feel this awful sensation crawl over my body like a pack of fleas. It felt like someone had thrown a bucket of ice cold water over my head. I turned around and gave Adira my most encouraging smile.

"Come on. It's not half-bad." Adira gave me yet another filthy look then took her first step inside too. I could see her wince as she comprehended just how cold we were going to be for the next couple of hours.

"I think we should turn left. I've got a really bad feeling about the right turning." It was true though. It felt really dodgy.

"Most of the time, you are completely and utterly wrong, but, this time, I think I can safely guarantee that you are correct," Adira agreed with me. What? Adira agreed with me? The world must be going mad.

"Okay then." I turned and started walking to the left, Adira following not far behind. A second later, we ran back screaming to the entrance, the backs of our trousers singed.

"Well done, Beryl." Adira leaned over panting hard and rested her hands on her knees.

"Well, excuse me, but if I'm not mistaken, you were agreeing with me not so long ago." Adira chose not to answer. Good. Whoever designed this maze had a seriously messed-up sense of humour. We were just nearly burnt to death.

Jesus, if this is just the beginning of the maze, I'd hate to know what the rest of the maze was going to be like. Unfortunately, I was going to have to find out very soon. There were probably going to be demons and devils flying around trying to suck out our souls through our mouths. Brrr, not a very pleasant thought. At all.

We carried on walking through about a million other tunnels, each step taking us closer to what could be our deaths. And I wasn't just being a drama queen. We were going deeper and deeper into the mountain with every turn of the tunnels we were following. The freezing temperature of the tunnels was bound to give me frostbite. Soon enough, I'd be able to break chunks of my frozen flesh off my arms. Gross. Occasionally, we'd come to dead ends and had to back track our steps.

"Okay Beryl. Seeing as you are such a frickin' genius, what do you propose we do now?" Adira asked me, biting her nails. If you ask me, even though she sounded really sarcastic and evil, she looked kind of . . . nervous. Huh?

Before I could ask her why she looked like she was about to enter Hell, I heard a sort of grunt up ahead. I had been looking down at my feet while walking, trying to protect my eyes from being burnt off, so I hadn't been paying much attention to what was up ahead of me. I lifted my head up slowly, dreading what I was going to see. Please, god, don't let it be my mother. If it was, I don't know what I would do—probably throw myself into the nearest fire.

Looming up in front of me was some kind of Sphinx. It had the head and bare chest of a woman, but that was where the human features ended. It had a long arching lion back that glistened in the dim light given off by the flaming torches strung onto the walls. It had massive unfurled wings held magnificently over its arched soft back. I would bet anything that the golden fur on its back was as soft as it looked.

I stared up at her in awe, my hanging mouth giving the impression that I was a clueless idiot who had no idea how on earth I had managed to get myself there. All in all, it was not a very good first impression for me at least.

"Hello," I squeaked out after an awkward silence. I mean, the women/lion/bird wasn't even wearing any clothes for god's sake. What do you expect me to do? Do a hula dance and sing opera? Nu-uh, that was so not going to happen.

The WLB (women/lion/bird) gave no sign that she even heard me. I could swear that this . . . thing wasn't even alive. It didn't even look like it was breathing. I stared at it for a couple more minutes.

After making sure that there was no breath coming out of its mouth, I took the teeniest step forward, so small that I barely moved. Unfortunately, WLB saw me even if Adira hadn't. WLB slowly stretched out from her crouch low on the ground and slowly turned her long magnificent body directly across the path.

Now that her fat ass was out of the way, I could see that there was an old-fashioned oak door with gold patterns carved into the wood. I know exactly what you're thinking. Why can't this stupid teenage girl just jump over WLB and run for it? Truth be told, that's what I had been thinking before I processed how large the Sphinx really was.

I glanced over at Adira; she seemed just as clueless as I was for once, but, unlike me, she was determined to hide that little fact from me and the rest of the world. Pfft, just in case she had forgotten, I am a mind reader. Although judging from the fact that I couldn't even hear a whisper of the Sphinx's thoughts, I couldn't nose in on mythical creature's thoughts—bummer. That meant I couldn't read any of my family's thoughts or Adira's.

"Um, I think we're supposed to solve a riddle?" Adira half said, half asked me. How am I supposed to know? I scored the worst history grade in my class.

"A riddle you have asked for, a riddle you shall get. Fail to answer and your life will be lost. Answer correctly and you will be allowed access to The Scroll of Elysium." The Sphinx spoke in a deep masculine voice that would suit the bogey monster way more than a WLB.

> *I have legs that keep me upright;*
> *I have a back that gives away comfort to those that use me,*
> *Yet I have no neck or a head.*
> *Young ones try to clamber onto me;*
> *Old ones need help to be lowered onto me;*
> *What am I?*

What the hell was this WLB blathering on about? She could have been talking about a fridge for all I knew. Yet for some reason, I didn't really get the impression that she was talking about a fridge.

All I wanted right now was a chair. Oh, a beautiful, luxurious chair. My back was aching, my feet were killing, me, and I had a headache that made me feel like molten lava was being poured through my ears and into my brain. I would give away my right arm and leg to be able to sit on a lovely, beautiful, gorgeous chair.

Jesus Christ. I am seriously losing my head right now. I'm going loony. Oh Christ. I really need to get more sleep with a chair right next to me, a pretty chair. Oh please, god, don't let me have a nervous breakdown because if I did, I would—hold on.

A chair has four legs and a back. And Carla used to always try and climb onto the chairs. How could I forget that? She used to always get slapped on the hand. And grandpa needs help to sit down in his chair. God knows I should know—I've always been the one yelled at, whatever it was I had been doing at that particular time, to help him into his chair. Even though I love grandpa to bits, it's not exactly enjoyable to put a phone call on hold while you helped your mother's father into his seat.

"It's a chair, Adira! It has to be! Just think about it!" Yes! I am a complete and utter genius if I do say so myself. Oh Adira's face was so funny. It looked like she was a constipated old woman trying to get rid of her waste in the toilet.

"Beryl . . . You do realise that if you are wrong for any reason, the price we will pay is with our own lives. Do you really think that I'm willing to put our lives on the line just because of one of your silly daydreams? Nuh-uh."

Spoilsport. She was only doing it because she couldn't stand the fact that, for once, I had gotten something right and she hadn't. Hadn't anyone ever told her that jealousy was not a good thing? Anyway, she didn't approve of my answer, even though I knew I was right. And I wasn't about to stand around with a cannibal mythical creature for one second longer.

"Um, ma'am? I've got the answer for your riddle." The Sphinx turned her head slowly to face me. Her large piercing eyes bored through mine. If looks could kill, I would've died right there on the spot. She said nothing.

"Is it a chair?" I asked, holding my breath. I didn't dare to look at Adira to gouge out her expression. I wanted to live long enough to find out if it was the correct answer. I could hear a loud swallow from behind me. My heart thudded as WLB still said nothing. What if I was wrong? Adira would make my death a living hell if I didn't end up there.

WLB stood up to her full magnificent height and reached for the large sword hanging by her waist. She slowly lifted it up into the air. Oh crap. I was wrong. I barely had time to close my eyes before I heard the swish and thud of the sword cutting through flesh and bone But not my flesh and bone—the Sphinx's. Huh?

I opened my eyes just in time to see the Sphinx fall down on her knees and on her side. The sword was plunged deep down slightly to the left of her chest where her heart supposedly was. The light in her eyes dimmed as she slowly withdrew from the world to wherever dead animals go.

She was dead. Great, I now had the death of a mythical creature on my conscience as well—terrific, absolutely smashing. I didn't know whether I should cavort around like a mad woman singing songs that we had beaten the WLB or have a two minute silence for it.

I looked at Adira and, instead, asked her the most obvious question. "Adira? Why did she kill herself?"

"Sphinxes kill themselves once their riddle has been solved. We better go now. You don't want to be in the same room as a mythical creature that has just died. Their ashes need to go to Roste, place for the dead mythical creatures. To do that, their bodies burn away, and their ashes will sink through the earth to the underworld," Adira said.

Well, thank you very much Ms. Encyclopaedia. Sure enough, the edges of WLB's hair looked like it was catching fire. I didn't know about Adira, but I didn't want to watch the body of a creature whose death I had caused burn away.

I practically ran to the oak door and pulled it open. I followed Adira who somehow ended up in front of me, into a round circular room full of shadows and pillars, even though there were no corners. I heard a voice say my name, a familiar voice.

"Hello, Adira. You would not believe how glad I am to see you today." My father said—my father?

"Dad?"

CHAPTER 12

My father walked out from behind one of the pillars that would make a hide and seek player ecstatic. Seriously, it was like the wall of China. You couldn't see across it. I am such a retard. I might as well have been thinking about flowers and rainbows in Hell; in other words, something completely inappropriate.

"Dad?" I said again. It was more a question. I was actually thinking, "What the Hell are you doing here? You're supposed to be dead in case you missed that tiny little fact." Obviously, with me being the wimp I am, I didn't say any of that aloud.

"Adira, sweetheart, my darling, I've missed you so much." Huh? In my memories, my father was nothing like the man that stood before me. For one thing, my dad actually took showers. The stench coming from him was unbearable. My mother could probably smell it from wherever she was.

The man started walking closer towards me. "Beryl, Don't listen to a word of what he's saying," Adira whispered hurriedly. "He's a Chineydu. Can't you see a faint green glow around his body? That shows he—" Adira was cut off as my "father" walked into hearing distance. Well, it would explain a lot if he was actually a dead possessed person, like the smell.

"Beryl, my precious jewel," He said again, as if reminding me that he was still there. There was no chance of me forgetting. He stank. I suddenly felt a rage so large and intense that I thought I was actually going to go alight like the Sphinx had done.

How dare this lonesome spirit thing dig up my father's dead body or whatever it was he did and possess him? Calling me precious jewel was the straw that broke the camel's back. And if that wasn't bad enough, he tried to make me believe that he, a stinky man who looked like my father, was my dad. Nuh-uh, that was so not going to happen.

"You're not my father," I hissed. "You're nothing like him. For one thing, he had showers. And he was dead the last time I checked."

"Beryl, Beryl, Beryl, your great sense of humour always gave away your ancestors, one particular ancestor anyway." My "father" clicked his fingers once, and his shadow seemed to come alive, like the shadows in the modern *Princess and the Frog*. It swooped down like an eagle and flew right through Adira's body like she wasn't even there. Adira's eyes bulged open in shock, and, slowly, she toppled down towards the floor.

I blinked and stood there with my mouth hanging wide open. You couldn't really blame me though. It's not exactly common to see your "friend" pass out in front of you. I could almost hear my Uncle Danny telling me to go to her and check that her brain hadn't fallen out through her ears. I almost smiled, but I held it in. Even a psycho wouldn't laugh at seeing one of their friends pass out.

"Yes, Beryl, I am not your father. I am Nathanial, the greatest sorcerer to have lived. It was I who defied death and found the way to live for all eternity. It was I who found the Scroll of Elysium unaided." Well, he certainly isn't ashamed to boast about how "amazing" he is.

"You're the one who sent me that thing on that website Adira gave me," I said musingly. I mean, I had guessed that ages ago, when I first found out that it was Nathanial who was looking for me, but I had to make sure. Yeah, I know, whatever, I could die any second; and I was concerned over who had sent me that weird thing on the computer?

"Yes, I thought it would add to the . . . suspense," he said delicately. "But that is not what matters now. The Scroll of Elysium is the most important thing at the moment."

"Yeah, well, why don't you just go and get it now?" I honestly wasn't trying to be sarcastic. I was just curious. I mean, if it had been me standing in the same room as the Scroll of Elysium, I would have been all over it the way Amy Winehouse used to be over drugs and alcohol (No offence Ms. Winehouse; wherever you are, I still love your songs.).

"Oh Beryl, I can see that you still have that sweet naivety that most children nowadays do not have. Do you really think that if it was as simple as that, I wouldn't have taken it by now?"—God, what an oily voice. Plus I am so not a child.

"Er . . . okay. But why don't you just go and get it now? What's stopping you?" I mean, my dad was no wrestler, but he was still a lot stronger than me. Plus, even if he didn't knock me out with a punch to the face, I would probably faint from the smell coming from him.

This body, which used to be my father's, had been dead for more than three months. It's hardly surprising that he would stink as much as he did.

"Beryl, believe me; if I could, I would have gotten it a long time ago." His voice had taken on a frustrated tinge. "But, unfortunately, I got things a little wrong. It seems that the Scroll of Elysium will come willingly only to those who are descendants of its creator— Aya. I did not anticipate that little fact."

Jesus. Is this man completely and utterly bonkers or what? How can a bunch of papers know whether we were related to an old dead woman unless it had an inbuilt DNA tester? And quite frankly, I never had a DNA test. Mother wouldn't let me. She thought someone would sell it online. And I'm guessing DNA scanners weren't invented when Aya was still alive.

"What would make you think that?" I was using my posh British accent.

"Look up."

I looked up at where the ceiling was supposed to be and saw a stream of stars swooping across the "ceiling." Above it, the night sky stretched on, even though I was pretty sure it was still daytime back in London. There were little winks every so often, like rain in sunlight. That's it. This man is either a wizard, or I was having loopy hallucinations.

"What . . . what is it?" I asked.

"It's the pathway to the Scroll of Elysium, Beryl, dear. These are Morphic stars. They change into whatever it is you designed it to protect. But it only opens to people of a certain . . . 'kind.' In this case, it only opens for the people who are descendants of Aya. This, Beryl, is what I need you for."

Wow. He actually sounds quite nice. If he was about a billion years younger and not my archenemy hiding inside my father's body, we could actually be friends. I know. Shocking—I'm actually considering a mass murderer being my friend, another sign that I was dropped on my head frequently as a child.

"I don't get it. How does a bunch of stars help you get the Scroll of Elysium?"

"Beryl, please use some of your foretold common sense to try and figure it out." His voice was still level and calm, but a burst of anger flared up in his eyes. It quickly vanished as he tried to calm himself down. Whoa. He had some major mood swings. I blame it entirely on PMS, except there was a slight problem with that theory. He wasn't a woman.

"The stars morph together to make the Scroll of Elysium. What you are seeing is the Scroll of Elysium in its most simple form. The stars will piece together to make the Scroll of Elysium. Now, do you understand?" His voice sounded as though it was a struggle for him to stop himself from getting a gun out and shooting my brains out.

"Yes, thank you. But what makes you think that I would help you?" I asked, turning slightly towards the door so I could run for it just in case. Yes, I know; whatever. I am a complete and utter coward.

"Because of this." Nathanial, my father, tugged on a rope tied around a pillar, and, slowly, a body came into view. His head was slumped forward like he had no energy to lift it. He didn't look familiar until he lifted his head.

My mouth dropped open. It was Ako. He had a rope tied around his lower face, giving a good excuse as to why he hadn't screamed yet.

"One click of my finger, and he'll be gone forever," Nathanial half-whispered like he was an actor in a horror movie. I give up. I don't even like Ako, but I didn't want to go around for the rest of my life with *another* death on my conscience.

"Okay, okay, whatever. You win, old man. Just tell me what you need me to do." Okay. My plan was to get the Scroll of Elysium, somehow, try to grab Adira and Ako at the same time, and run. I know exactly what you're thinking. What is this girl on? I know it's not much good, but it was the only thing I could think of.

"Look at the stars, and close your eyes. Imagine every star fusing together to make the Scroll of Elysium. Imagine yourself reaching out a hand and plucking it out from the sky. Then give it to me." Okay. It sounds simple enough. Unfortunately, it wasn't as easy as Nathanial had said it was. On the contrary, it was near impossible.

I closed my eyes and took a deep breath in. As soon as I closed my eyes, I immediately thought of daises and buttercups, and picnics in the spring. If you haven't figured it out by now, that wasn't exactly what I was supposed to be thinking about. And, as if by a miracle, Nathanial sussed that I wasn't doing what he had told me to.

"Beryl, you are not concentrating enough. If you do not put your full energy and mind into merging the Scroll of Elysium, I will be forced to do something that I do not wish to do."

Crikey. He sounded as though he was threatening to kill me! With that thought in mind, I closed my eyes again.

I thought of the Scroll of Elysium . . . being pieced back together again. There's no other way to explain what I was doing. And, somehow, it worked.

Imagine a jigsaw puzzle. The whole picture wouldn't be complete until every piece was joined together. That's a bit like the Scroll of Elysium. Each piece was made to fit together, but you couldn't force the wrong pieces together. It wouldn't fit and, in the end, be damaged. Just like the Scroll of Elysium.

I opened one eye and slowly opened the other as I realised what it was I was seeing—the Scroll of Elysium. It was spinning around lazily in the air above Nathanial's head as if it couldn't be bothered to rotate itself. Nathanial's (or my father's) face was alight with glee. That couldn't have been a good thing for me. As life goes, if the baddie is happy, the goodie is sad, and if the goodie is happy, then the baddie is sad. Same goes for my family.

"Give it to me, Beryl, dear." Gee, now that Nathanial/my father could actually see the Scroll of Elysium, his voice changed. It instantly became oilier than ever if that was even possible.

"How do I do that? For one thing, I am definitely not going to be able to reach. And second, you can't either."

"No, you stupid girl, imagine the Scroll of Elysium slowly floating down in the air towards the palm of your outstretched hand. Imagine it landing softly and safely in the comfort of your hand." Whoa. It looks like we have a reincarnation of Shakespeare on board.

I closed my eyes once again and did exactly what he told me to do like I was some sort of slave, and he was the evil Egyptian master who would whip me if I didn't do exactly as he told me. I stretched out my hand, and instantly felt the lightest thing land on it.

I opened my eyes, not quite understanding that I had the legendary Scroll of Elysium in my hand. It felt so papery and old as though it would rip if I breathed too hard on it.

"Yes, Beryl, that's it. Now, give it to me and everything will be all right." He was half whispering now, as if he was scared that he would somehow ruin it by talking too loud.

I paused, helpless, not knowing what to do. If I gave it to him, I would have a better chance of living; but he would destroy the world or whatever you want to call it, and I would still end up dead, one way or another.

I closed my eyes *again* and tried to think what Aya would do if she was in my situation. I felt a light flowery breeze touch my face, almost caressing me. I opened my eyes, half-praying that it wasn't Nathanial touching my face. Maybe that was his evil plan: try and make me throw up and give him a free path to the Scroll of Elysium.

But it didn't *smell* like him. Nathanial smelled of rotting fish, and this smelled more . . . floral.

Something behind Nathanial caught my attention. It looked as though there was something standing behind him. It didn't look human—it looked as though if you blew on it, it would vanish.

It looked a lot like . . . Aya. She opened her mouth and said in a hushed voice, *"Beryl . . . I have faith in you, dear one . . ."* I blinked, and when I opened my eyes, she wasn't there anymore. Maybe she hadn't even been over there. Maybe I was losing my mind.

But what on earth was I was supposed to do? The most logical thing for me to do in my opinion is to hang on to it for as long as possible. And the way to do so is by doing my favourite thing in the whole wide world—talking.

"So, Nathanial, what exactly is it you want to do with the Scroll of Elysium?" I asked, inwardly cursing myself for asking the stupidest thing possible to the evil mastermind of the last couple of centuries. Make that millenniums.

"That, Beryl, is only for me to know and you to dream about. Now, give it to me, Beryl, before I am forced to do something that I will eventually regret doing."

I stopped moving, now completely clueless as to what to do. Nathanial, clearly bored of waiting for me to give him the Scroll of Elysium, walked forward towards me, one slow step after another.

The best thing I could think of was holding my breath. He slowly reached out his right hand and left it gently resting on the Scroll of Elysium. I could barely breathe by now. All I could think of doing was giving him some of the old cologne that Dad never got around to using. Now would be the best time for him to use it.

All I could think of doing was getting his hand off the Scroll of Elysium before he managed to take it from me. I knew that if he took it from me now, I would never get it back. I grabbed his wrist and tried to pull it away from the Scroll of Elysium. He gave out a strangled scream as though I was burning him alive.

I felt the weirdest sensation as though I was actually Nathanial, and I could see images from his life coming in a long stream of memories and flashbacks. I saw a young boy with a mop of dark hair resting on the top of his head as though he was wearing a loose fitting wig, sitting in a dark corner of a room. Images, one after another, came pouring into my mind.

From the dazed look on Nathanial's face, I could see that he was probably seeing the same things as me. I saw an unfamiliar-looking man holding hands with Aya. I saw them laughing together. I saw a woman smiling and hugging the same boy as before, only older, and congratulating him for doing something.

They came on and on, one after another. I probably wouldn't have let go of him, but then I got the shock of my life. I saw Adira and Nathanial together. Only it wasn't a normal picture.

Adira was down on the floor with a massive gash on her forehead. Her whole face was swollen and puffy, as if she had been hit repeatedly on the head. She looked dead. Nathanial was looking down at her with the unmistakeable expression of glee painted on. He looked mental. I let go of his arm in shock.

I stared at him, suddenly feeling more scared than I had ever been in my whole life. If he was capable of hurting Adira like that, then there was no saying what he would do to me, a virtual stranger.

He was still moaning in pain as though I had somehow hurt him. That was when I noticed the smell of burning flesh.

I looked down slowly at what used to be his arm. There was practically nothing there now. You could see more bone than flesh. It was smoking slightly as though he had actually been burnt by me. The little flesh remaining was all wasted and grey like the mummies in *The Mummy Returns*. It was not a pretty sight. I was definitely going to have to have some serious retail therapy to get over this.

"What are you?" he asked me in exactly the same way as people in movies do. But, seeing as this was me I was talking about, I didn't come out with the usual *"I am Beryl Jones."* Instead, I said so utterly wittingly, "I'm not sure to be honest."

It was true at least. I certainly wasn't your average human being, but I certainly wasn't a monster or alien either. I hope. I suddenly felt stronger as though I had a chance of making it out of there alive. "Sorry father for what I am about to do," I said in my head.

I lounged forward and, holding my breath, grabbed hold of his head. I closed my eyes, almost drowning in my mind as different images from Nathanial's life swamped me. I saw many things as I held on to Nathanial's face while he screamed and writhed in pain under me. Okay, that sounds wrong.

Anyhow I saw so many things that I would never expect to see from my sister, let alone my arch enemy. I saw him playing by some sort of river with a group of kids, and each and every one of them looked so innocent and carefree that it was hard to believe that one of them would turn out to be a mass murderer.

I saw a young man who was probably Nathanial standing over a sickly-looking woman who closed her eyes with a little sigh. The last breath she would ever take. I felt a sense of loss even though I was probably watching the mother of my biggest (and only) enemy dying. That's how you know I've definitely got problems.

Every single thing I saw after I saw his mother allegedly dying was of him planning on doing something bad, doing something bad, or revelling in having done something bad—not a good look for women.

I could feel myself slowly getting fainter and fainter as the last of my strength gave out, but not once did I remove my hands from what used to be Nathanial's face. I somehow knew, even in my tipsy state, that if I moved my hands, I wouldn't have a hope of ever seeing sunlight again.

The last thing I saw before I passed out was a large pile of ashes on the floor. Great, I had just cremated my own father using just my hands. What a daughter I turned out to be.

*   *   *

I opened my eyes slowly, each eyelid feeling like it weighed a ton. No joke. I could smell something that smelled oddly like Ambrosia and antibacterial wipes combined. But that can't have been possible. The only place I know of that would have Ambrosia is Morpheus. But—oh no, I was back in Morpheus.

"She's awake!" I heard the unmistakeable voice of Adira practically shriek. It's nice to know that they all have the health of my eardrums in mind. I sat up in the bed which I appeared to be lying in, blinking the stars and moons out of my vision.

When my vision had cleared up, I could see that I was in a cubicle of some sort with curtains drawn around them. Adira was sitting on my left and Ako on my right, both of them looking completely unscathed, except for the fact that they had various bruises on their arms and faces from what I could see of them.

"Wha— . . . what happened?" I croaked, completely forgetting that they were both knocked out for most of the time I was with Nathanial. "Well, that's something only you can tell us," Ako said, his voice sounding as though he had been gargling nails.

"Yes, I know; but, after I passed out, surely, you have at least some idea as to what happened." Well, sorry for wanting to know what I had missed in my life. Plus I wasn't bound to be in the greatest mood after I had had to cremate my own father and pass out twice in one day.

"I came round after you passed out. I'm not sure how long you were unconscious for, but I knew that there was something wrong with you. For one thing, you looked kind of blue. Ako was still knocked out, so I created a portal so that I could take you and Ako back to Morpheus. And here we are now. Now, you have some serious explaining to do. Start from just after I . . . passed out."

Clearly, they do not care that I have just been through a traumatic time in my life. I could have just been bombed by the Taliban, and they would still want to know everything that they did not know.

With a sigh, I set myself the task of explaining every single little detail of the last twenty-four hours that they did not know about.

They listened, their eyes getting wider and wider as I told them what had happened. By the time I finished, I was seriously worried that their eyes would pop out of their sockets. They both leaned back to their chairs at exactly the same time. It would've been funny, but I wasn't exactly in a laughing mood. Plus I myself had some questions that needed answering.

"But I don't get it. How come, when I touched Nathanial, his face literally burnt away? I mean, I'm pretty sure I don't have any hidden fire powers. Or do I?" I asked, not really directing my question at either of them.

"It's because he's a Chineydu. You already know what a Chineydu is, don't you?" Ako asked me. I nodded silently. "Well, Chineydus cannot touch living flesh without them burning away. It's like they can't handle the feeling of living flesh, and the older a Chineydu is, the more they are used to being in dead bodies with no circulation and working organs. Nathanial was a very old Chineydu, far older than Chineydus are meant to exist. That is why he burnt away immediately. Do you get what I mean?" I nodded again, like I was some sort of nodding China figure.

"Why did I see Nathanial's whole life though? I mean, I don't think that's exactly normal is it?"

"No, Beryl. Clearly, it is not," Adira piped in like she couldn't bear to keep her mouth closed for a minute longer. I'm not surprised really. It was only a matter of time before she found a way to include herself in me and Ako's conversation. "It's just your mind-reading skills and your psychic skills merged together. It gave you the ability to see Nathanial's past." Even though it was left unsaid between us, I knew that she knew that I knew what he had done to her.

"Oh, crap," I whispered under my breath. I just realised that I hadn't asked the most important question. Where was the Scroll of Elysium? I voiced my question to Ako and Adira, feeling panic-stricken. I had passed out, cremated my own father's body using my bare hands, and been to Hell and back, all for nothing. Why me?

"It's completely vanished. No one knows where it is. It could be on a different planet for all we know. All we know is that it can't be used to harm us anymore," Ako replied.

I was just about to ask him how he had ended up with Nathanial in the first place but then thought better of it. That, I could ask another time. For now, I was satisfied with the answers I had gotten. And now, I was going to try and get some well-earned sleep, which I deserved, even if I do say so myself.

But there was still one thing that I did not understand.

"What . . . There's one thing I still don't get. Why did my father tell me not to trust my mother when she turned out to be one of the good guys?" I asked, suddenly alert.

"Well, Nathanial possessed your mother for a while to get more information about you. Nathanial barely knew anything about you, so I'm guessing he wanted to know your weaknesses before he made any attempt to attack you," Adira replied.

"So that's how he gave me that locket," I said more to myself than to Adira or Ako. Well, I had to give it to Nathanial. He certainly never rushed into decisions. He really had thought of everything. Pity I burnt him to death though. He and my mother would have made great friends. Just as I was thinking of evil twisted creatures, a sharp voice cut through my thoughts.

"Beryl!" A high-pitched voice that sounded very familiar to me drifted towards me like it was some sort of curse. It was Ms. Sparks—so much for getting a good night's sleep. I'd be lucky if I slept for ten minutes straight without being shaken awake for one thing or another.

Ms. Sparks walked into the room half-smiling, as if she knew that she had just stopped me from doing something that I loved doing—sleeping. It was going to be a long time before I got any sleep, just my luck.

THE AUTHOR

Aida Getachew was born in 1999 in London, United Kingdom, where she lives with her parents, younger sister and brother. Her parents are originally from Ethiopia.

Aida attended Roe Green Infant and Junior Schools and is currently in year 9 at Kingsbury High School. Aida wrote her first novel, SECRETS OF LIFE, when she was only twelve years old.